ERICKA EVREN

MISSION OF THE RO'ARCK

ARCHARIAN SERIES - BOOK 1

Dedication

To God.
Thank you for Your steady hand upon my life and for the gift of grace.

For my dad.
Thank you for your encouragement and for always believing in me.

Also by Ericka Evren

Archarian series
Mission of the Ro'arck
Echoes of Destiny
Rise of Legends

Spin offs
Trials of Honor

Short Stories
Fugitive of the Stars – Honor a Sci-Fi & Fantasy Anthology

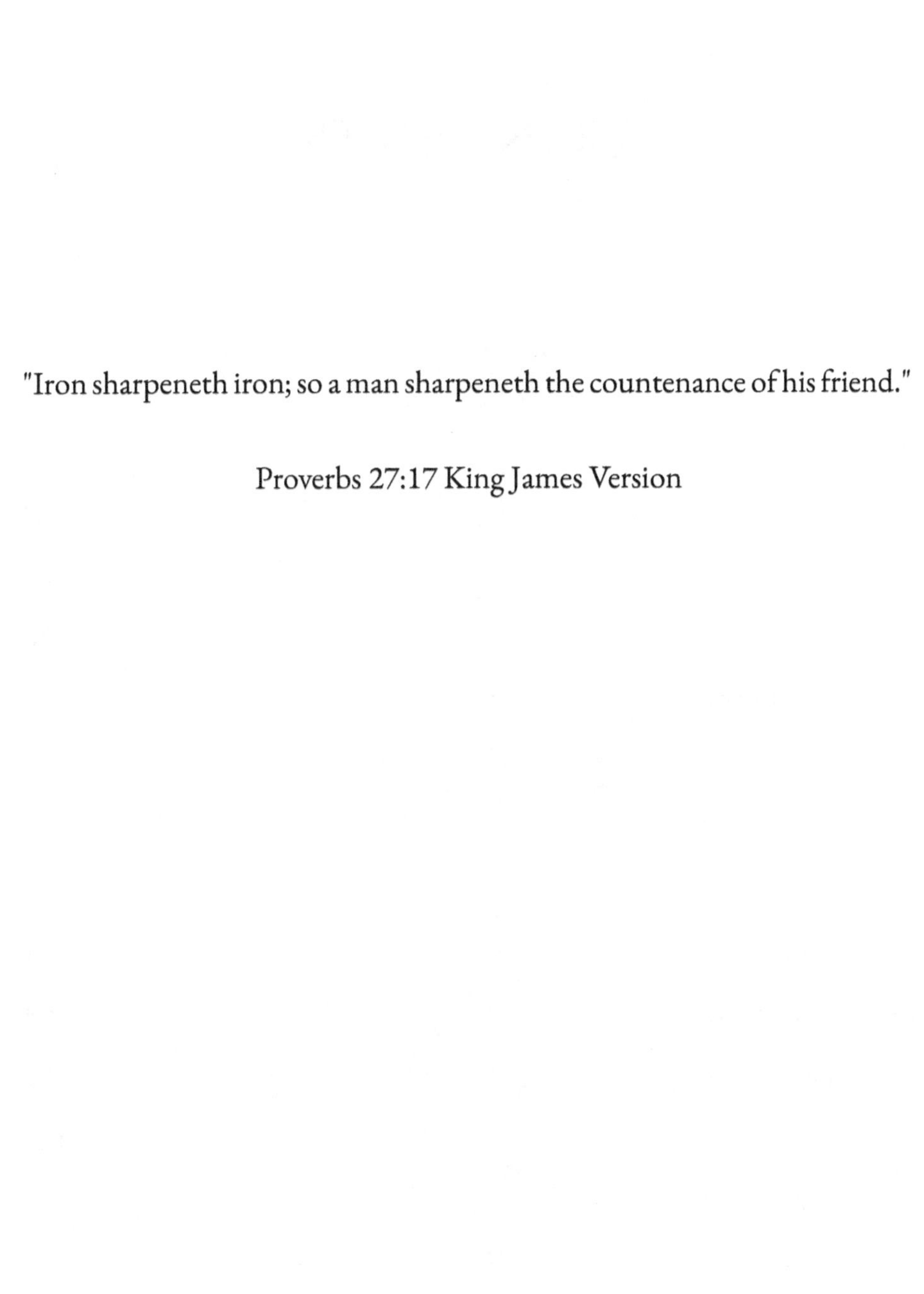

"Iron sharpeneth iron; so a man sharpeneth the countenance of his friend."

Proverbs 27:17 King James Version

CONTENTS

Key Terms

Archaria: The planet of the Archarians. A race with superior technology in the galaxy.

Arkross: A device created by the Archarians that allows instantaneous travel from one world to the next via bent time and space.

Solar rotation: The definition of one year for the people of Archaria.

Rotation: The definition of one day for the people of Archaria.

Creative Clan: One of the three clans of Archaria that specializes in the creative arts whether technological or artistic.

Farmer Clan: One of the three clans of Archaria that specializes in growing crops and tending to animals. Regarded as the lowest clan.

Warrior Clan: One of the three clans of Archaria that specializes in rigorous physical and cognitive development for battle and operation of starships. Regarded as the most respected clan.

The council: The council comprises three appointed members by the civilians of Avsilan. Each council member is a representative of their respective clan, Warrior, Creative, or Farmer.

Avsilan: The capitol city of Archaria.

Grand Tower: The capitol building of Avsilan where the arkross is kept, the Warrior clan has their command center, and all meetings with the members of the alliance take place.

Ranks: The highest to lowest as follows. General officers: admiral, vice admiral; senior officers: captain, commander, lieutenant-commander, lead operator; junior officers: lieutenant, sub-lieutenant, acting sub-lieutenant;

subordinate officer: cadet.

Narvent: A station near Archaria that facilitates the refueling of starships and performing extensive repairs. A lead operator oversees the coming and going of vessels and manages it.

Drorse: Horse-fox-like creature that inhabits the mountainous regions of Archaria.

Chapter 1

KAYTRIX

Kaytrix gazed across the open, sunny fields of the alien world, Drenna. The farmers he protected tended to their crops in the heat of the late afternoon. He knew the toll gardening had on one's body, having grown up as a farmer's son. It could be him breaking a sweat over the rows, but instead he stood there as a protector.

He decided early in his life to join the Warrior clan to avoid that kind of labor, but now all he did was stand here. Life was easy standing, but that was the problem. He *hated* being idle.

One hundred and eighty planetary rotations passed since he had arrived, with no sign of the pirates since their first raid. What a way to be cheated.

The humid planet became too much to endure. He slouched, trying to find relief from the sticky armor he wore.

"Look sharp, Lieutenant Torex!" his superior barked through his comm. "Unless you want to join them?"

Kaytrix straightened as snickers swept through the soldiers. "Cut it out, Ryll." He glared at the man under his command and tightened his fist. Ryll always tried to rile him up, as if he enjoyed the tension. Could he blame him? There wasn't much to do but poke fun.

"That's enough," Lieutenant Commander Rev'd said.

Ryll rolled his eyes and turned his body toward Duke, another soldier in his squad.

Sweat trickled along Kaytrix's brow, irritating him. He glanced to where Lieutenant Commander Rev'd stood in the watchtower, desiring nothing more than to make a quip. He resisted the urge. His temper had gotten him into trouble before. That's why he remained a lieutenant and hadn't ranked up.

Being stationed here was both a punishment and a test. He knew it had everything to do with him decking his last superior officer, but the man had it coming. He could only take grating of his origins for so long before he snapped.

Officers of the Warrior clan had a distaste for those who originated from the Farmer clan. This mission was just another attempt to force him out, but he wasn't caving. He'd take all the shitty assignments in a heartbeat.

This was his dream, but more than that, this was his only opportunity to earn enough pieces to pay for his ma's expensive medical bills. With his father taking care of her, there was no one to run the farm and earn income. He needed to support them, and he couldn't do that if he continued to let others get under his skin.

So, he bit his tongue, tried to obey his superiors, and endured ridicule from fellow squad members—anything he could do to stay. The moment he allowed himself to slip, the admirals could revoke his right to be part of the Warrior clan. The council would force him to farm fields for the rest of his life and he would never earn enough to take care of his family.

He scoffed. He'd try to join the Creative clan if that ever happened.

"Something funny, soldier?" Rev'd asked through the comm in his ear.

He flinched. "No, sir!" he replied. "Just a fly in my nose, sir!"

Another round of snickers echoed in his ears. He ignored the men as he gazed out across the green fields again. Could his childhood dream of commanding his own ship ever come true? Everything so far told him it was impossible.

He itched for some action, heck, a *lot* of action. Standing here drained his will to live and part of him prayed for the pirates to return.

The farmers left the field as the last ray of bright red-orange light settled below the horizon of dirt. He readied to leave his post, slinging his weapon over his back. He waited for the coming order to switch with another squad.

A moment passed. Darkness settled. The town's glow illuminated the field and the other men who stood with him, waiting. His armor stifled him. He glanced to his gauntlet: no messages.

Rev'd was late announcing their rotation.

It took every ounce of his control to resist activating his comm. He glanced at the other soldiers in his squad as they shifted weight from one leg to another. One huffed audibly across the field. Even they were at their patience's end.

Lieutenant Rev'd never delivered orders late. Was it another way to make him suffer? Just as the heat became intolerable, his comm activated.

"Lieutenant Torex," Lieutenant Commander Rev'd said, his words rushed. "Return to base camp at once. We have received orders for your squad to be reassigned effective immediately. Head to the arkross for transport."

"Affirmative, Lieutenant Commander."

Did Rev'd know where they were going? He wanted to ask but it didn't matter. He could finally say goodbye to this dust bowl.

A chorus of whoops and hurrahs echoed through his comm as his squad received the same orders. As he turned to head back to base, doubt slithered in. What if where they were going was worse than this place?

Kaytrix put his doubts aside, rallied his men, and squared up in front of the arkross. The huge arched device stood like a massive gate, tethering worlds together with the ability to transport matter from one planet to another. Etched upon its frame were symbols unique to the culture who created it: the Archarians, his ancestors. It was one of their finer creations as a race, no matter how ancient the gates were.

He admired the device for a second, a wave of zeal coursing through his veins. He couldn't wait for the energy to flow through him and whisk him home.

Someone shoved his back. He turned to see Ryll sneering.

"What did you do now?" Ryll snickered, turning to Duke to fist bump.

Kaytrix shook his head. Why couldn't Ryll just be happy and leave him alone? "I asked to be reassigned so I wouldn't have to put up with your snoring."

"Ooo." The remark came from Duke, his round lips a small hole in his big head.

Ryll's face crumpled, and he crossed his arms.

Kaytrix turned. Maybe he had a chance of gaining their respect after all. He waited in the ever-growing humidity of the evening, contemplating their next assignment. Would there be pirates to fight this time? Perhaps the admiral would station them on a starship? He couldn't wait for some action, but hoped to have time to wash the sweat and dirt from his body before being dispatched to another world.

Lieutenant Commander Rev'd approached from the left, slapping a hand across his back.

"Maybe I will see you and your squad again, eh Lieutenant Torex?"

"Not on your life." He grimaced. He could live his entire life without coming back here.

Rev'd laughed, but his beady eyes betrayed his jealousy for their departure. "Best of luck, *farmer.* Report to the imperial guards upon your arrival."

The arkross activated with a swirl of blue energy, creating a sphere of bent time and space. Lieutenant Commander Rev'd saw them off with a quick salute—a fist slammed to his heart.

"Get out of here, you lucky bastards."

Kaytrix nodded in recognition as they stepped onto the arkross and disappeared through the glowing sphere. The energy kissed his skin with soft electrical zaps, a sensation he wasn't used to yet.

Once through the portal, Kaytrix stepped down the arkross steps, trying to catch his breath from the instant travel. While using the portal was convenient, it left him feeling odd. He much preferred traveling by ship.

An arched ceiling encapsulated the arkross in a secure round room. A single doorway to his left led farther into the building where pillars and walls of stone stood. Every several paces, a banner of the Archarian crest hung: three mountain peaks representing truth, peace, and unity. This was the Great Tower of the Archarian capitol, Avsilan.

As the last of his squad joined him, two Archarian imperial guards approached.

"Lieutenant Torex," one welcomed. His blue armor shimmered in the light of the deactivating arkross. "We are here to escort you to your temporary quarters until the admiral is ready for you. This way, please."

Kaytrix gestured his men to follow and took point, absorbing details of the Great Tower. Pillars, extravagant staircases, glass windows, and bright light embodied the spirit of Archarian culture.

Kaytrix never tired of the reverence. The structure represented his heritage and epitomized the accomplishments of his race. The Great Tower facilitated peaceful gatherings between their allies and the council, and housed their military command center. Everyone on Archaria, regarded Avsilan as the leading city because of this fine structure.

Even though he appreciated the grandeur of the building, he couldn't ignore his growing need for an icy shower. Each step chafed his body.

The imperial guard led them to lower area of the tower where rows of barracks housed soldiers during their travels between planets.

"We will contact you when it is time to report to Admiral Ackon. Until then, get some rest," said the guard. He saluted and left.

Duke surged forward. "I call dibs on—"

"Not so fast, Duke!" Kaytrix stuck his arm across the soldier's chest. "As your commanding officer, I get to pick first."

Duke groaned.

Kaytrix pointed to a single bunk room on the far left. "That's mine. You guys can pick what you want."

His filthy squad took off howling, shoving, and pushing each other out of the way as they fought for top or bottom bunk. Seems no one had considered the quality of a good shower.

The rooms were small but provided adequate amenities. His was especially small, but an agreeable change from having to share with the men. He closed the door to his chambers and removed the armor he'd been sweating in for so long.

He took his time soaking in the icy water of the shower. The chill pressed an invisible reset button and he relaxed.

The water drained at his feet, taking with it the filth of dirt, heat, and frustration. He waved his hand across the shower panel and the flow of water ceased followed by a dry air.

Now he needed to prep to see the admiral. He would go alone while his squad rested. As much as they made fun of him, he was grateful for them. Being back home, though, only brought to the surface memories of his old academy companions, Nat, Drozah, and Mac. They were like his siblings since they had grown up and attended basic education together. After graduation and initiation into their respective roles, he had lost touch with them. Where were they after these ten long solar rotations?

He still couldn't believe it had been that long. Ten solar rotations . . .

Buzz, buzz.

Kaytrix's comm rattled on the countertop. He snatched it, carefully placed it into his ear, and tapped it once.

"Lieutenant Torex here," he said.

"Lieutenant Torex," a guard said. "The admiral will see you now. I trust you know your way to the command center?"

"Yes, thank you," he said.

The moment the communication ended, he scrambled to get ready. He did not expect to be summoned so soon. He struggled to dress, stumbling across the room in his under-armor to the suit-cleansing chamber. He struggled with his shirt as it stuck to his wet body.

"Shit." He groaned as he pulled his shirt down. He couldn't afford to be late.

He rushed out of his chambers to the nearest lift. Nerves bubbled in his chest as he selected the command center on the inside touch panel. Why had they been called back home so quickly? Had he proven himself to get a promotion?

A promotion meant he could pay for more of his ma's medical bills. He'd only been able to send a little of his earnings last time, the rest confiscated due to his assault on a commanding officer. If he couldn't pay for his ma's medicine, she would continue to grow ill.

The lift stopped at its destination level and opened its doors. Kaytrix rushed through, his shoulder striking a fellow officer on the way out.

"Sorry!" he called, ruffling his wet hair.

He approached the command center—another room built into the frame of the tower. The entrance was dark. Several consoles lit the dim space before him, their colors reflecting on the marble floor and lighting the faces of those nearby. Through the blur of a holographic screen, several vice admirals gathered around a holographic projection. They stood in silence as they studied it.

Kaytrix entered, saluted, and waited for the admiral.

Soft murmurs from the military personnel floated through the room. He could feel the tension as they spoke, quiet and urgent, the worry in their faces amplified by the shadows the light couldn't reach.

"Lieutenant," an older voice said. "I am surprised to see you still in service."

The insult cut deep. Would they ever end? He was a soldier, willing to serve. The marks he earned were proof enough. Still, the leaders of the Warrior clan regarded him as a farmer and nothing else.

"Yes, sir. Trying hard not to repeat my mistakes, sir." He struggled to see the admiral through the dimly lit space.

"Good, because where I am sending you there are no room for mistakes," Admiral Ackon said as he strode into the dim light of a hologram.

The admiral grimaced. Was his hair still wet?

"Admiral Ackon, agreeable to see you," Kaytrix said, saluting.

"At ease, Lieutenant. We have little time to discuss your next mission."

Kaytrix relaxed his stance.

"We are sending you and your squadron to the O'ber planet. It is a system on the cusp of Dexsortes."

That was the edge of the galaxy, where nothing ever happened. If they needed him there, it was something big.

"More pirates, sir?"

With an irritated look, the admiral pointed at the holographic display of the planet. "A territorial issue, nothing major. You and your squad will arrive tomorrow and report to Captain Wesk. He will have further instructions for you."

Kaytrix saluted again, excitement rushing through his veins. "Yes, sir."

"Oh, and we are no longer withholding any of your earnings. The next payment you receive will be the full amount."

A tension he was holding lifted from his shoulders. The news meant he could send more pieces to his family. "Thank you, sir."

"That is everything, Lieutenant." Ackon returned the salute and joined the vice admirals.

Kaytrix turned on his heel and bit the back of his hand, trying to curb his excitement as he left the command center. Finally, he would get a taste of some action. It was long coming.

Chapter 2
BATTLE OF O'BER

Kaytrix awoke to rapid thudding on his door.

"Hey, Lieutenant. Are you awake? We're ready to go!"

He recognized Ryll's voice and pictured his square jaw and menacing eyebrows. "Yes, I am," he grumbled, swinging his legs over the cot. "I'll be out in a minute. Find yourselves something to eat. We'll meet at the arkross shortly."

The squadron's excited voices faded, and his mind raced with possibility as he recalled yesterday's conversation.

Since he had shared the news with his squad, their excitement had been infectious. As recent graduates of the Military Academy, they desired nothing more than to flex their honed abilities. But no one wanted this more than he did.

Being raised in the Farmer clan made him feel as though he had more to prove than those born to a Warrior clan or a Creative clan. Some hated him more when he earned the Warrior mark. Mostly the clans got along alright, but the Warrior and Creative always viewed the Farmer clan as inferior. Whether the stigma came from them tilling the ground and not advancing their world, he wasn't sure.

The soldiers and leaders of Archaria would always think of him as inferior unless he could do something great to make the Warrior clan members forget his past. It was part of the reason he'd always dreamed of commanding his own starship. It was his hope this new mission could be his chance to earn the respect of his fellow Archarian officers.

Kaytrix glanced to his timekeeper. He had a moment to send his parents a quick update before he left. They'd want to know about this exciting mission and the release of his funds.

He settled into the chair and accessed the complimentary holo-screen communication display. With a few memorized strokes, he inputted the corresponding digits that would connect to his parents' terminal in their house.

A chime sung and he waited. The dark screen before him lit up and his father's face appeared looking far too close to his display.

"Hello? Hello? Who's calling the Torex household?" his father asked, eyeing the camera.

Kaytrix couldn't keep himself from chuckling. "It's me, Kaytrix. I have some news. Is Ma there?"

His father backed from the screen and a smile split across his face. "Ah, my boy! So, it is you. I'm afraid your ma is sleeping. She hasn't been doing well since they stationed you on that planet." His shoulders slumped and Kaytrix could see that taking care of his sick ma was affecting his father's health.

"I'm hoping to change that. Admiral Ackon himself reassigned me to another planet. Sounds like there will be plenty of action."

His father nodded. "Good, good. Hopefully its climate is more comfortable than the last planet."

Kaytrix chuckled. "Yeah. Oh, and guess what? I can send more pieces this time around for ma's medicine."

His father smiled again and this time, tears threatened to breach his aging eyes. "Why Kaytrix, that . . . that . . ." he stammered. He ran his hands over his face.

Kaytrix held his emotions in check.

"She's getting bad. This is a divine intervention." His father folded his hands and closed his eyes.

"I will transfer the funds right now. Tell Ma the good news for me, will you?" he asked.

"I will, son. We're both so proud of you. Try to stay out of trouble on this next mission, though." He let out a chuckle. "You get your temper from your ma."

Kaytrix rolled his eyes. "Yes, I know. I will chat with you soon. I must go now. Take care."

His father gave a little wave. "Bye now."

Kaytrix deactivated his hologram and grabbed his gear from the floor. By now the squad would be ready to go, but was he? Reiterating his excitement for the mission to his father caused a nervousness to boil in his gut. He'd never faced real action before, just simulations. He didn't know if he was ready for the real thing.

He took in a deep breath. He didn't have time to be nervous. It was time to be a lieutenant of the Archarian army, not a cowardly farm boy. He had all the training he needed to succeed at his mission, from ground combat to commanding a starship. Everyone did to graduate the academy. Now it was a matter of putting experience behind his training to rise in the ranks.

He left the barracks and took the lift to the main level of the Grand Tower that held the arkross. As he exited the lift, his squad came into view across the Grand Hall. They were smiling and joking loudly, but quieted as he regrouped with them.

"Hey, sleepyhead," Duke teased.

Kaytrix grimaced. "Save your brain power for the mission," he scolded with a half smile.

The others crooned in fun mockery.

"Someone's cranky," Ryll said.

Kaytrix glanced over each of them to make sure everyone was present. "Ready, men?" he asked, lifting an eyebrow.

They settled, their smiling faces replaced by stone. "Yes, sir!" they called out in unison.

He turned and entered the arkross room and nodded toward the imperial guards. "Permission to activate the arkross and proceed with our orders?"

One guard touched a fist to his heart. "Yes, Lieutenant. The arkross is ready for your departure."

Kaytrix searched his gauntlet for the coordinates in his mission file and selected the planet, O'ber. The planet floated above his gauntlet in a hologram and provided an option to continue or to decline. Pressing the hologram, he accepted the activation of the arkross.

The large device that once stood quiet came alive with a hum. The coordinates for the O'ber planet dialed into the device. Energy flowed from the center and to the arms, creating the portal. An enormous crystal connecting the arms together at the top beamed a bright blue. It flashed as this arkross created a connection to the arkross on the other side of the galaxy.

"Here we go, boys," Kaytrix uttered, his gaze locked on the forming sphere ahead of them.

In moments, the sphere formed as a hurricane, swirling inside its frame. Through it, they could see blurred images of light and shadows from the other side.

His heart sped faster. "Move out!" he ordered, leading his squadron through the portal.

He stepped off the platform and onto new ground. Rain drenched everything it touched, creating a fine, sloppy soup of soil. A campsite stood before them, doused by rain and splattered by mud. The trails appeared as deepened bogs. The only way the buildings remained standing was the firm foundations beneath them.

Men hurried past them in a frenzy, their arms full of ammunition. They struggled to keep upright on the terrain that threatened their balance. Multiple explosions sounded in the distance and missiles whistled through the damp air, their impacts shaking the planet's surface.

An officer stood boldly in the rain, giving orders. Kaytrix took a step forward and the squad followed behind, keeping close. He approached the commanding officer and saluted.

"Lieutenant Torex reporting for duty, sir! Captain Wesk is expecting us."

The dull eyes of the officer surprised him. The man looked aged, worn, whittled away by sleepless nights and fear.

A chill ran through Kaytrix as their eyes locked. Seeing defeat in a man's face wasn't something he saw before—least of all, seeing it in an Archarian's face.

"He's in command just over that ridge," the man said, rain dripping off his nose and over his thin lips.

Kaytrix nodded his thanks and motioned his men forward. He led them through the camp.

They passed the medical center when a strong odor filled his nostrils. Doctors knelt over injured men, desperate to stop bleeding. Others rushed around, scrounging for supplies, while wounded soldiers covered in their own blood waited for help.

One nurse sat in the rain outside the tent, her face pale with shock and smeared with blue blood from the soldiers. It seemed obvious extensive training did little to prepare her for the gruesome reality of conflict. Her ghostly stare left a hole in Kaytrix's soul as if it prophesied their fate.

As he shook off the imprint her gaze left on him, a group of soldiers carrying torches cut in front of his path. He was about to gripe at them when he caught himself, watching the fire sizzle in resistance to the downpour.

Rain tapped against his armor as he waited for them to pass. Curious, he looked ahead to their destination. What was their hurry? Deep within, something jarred his soul.

On the outskirts of the camp lay a heaped pile with oddly formed shapes poking out here and there. He was confused. Wet wood couldn't burn in this downpour. Then the wind came, and with it the sting of rain and the realization that this wasn't a brush pile, but the mangled bodies of fallen

Archarian soldiers. His heart sank. The soldiers who had cut him off were to dispose of them with fire.

There were too many.

Too many to bury.

Too many to take back home.

This was worse than a mere territorial issue. It was war.

Deep within himself, the ugly head of fear rose. The farther in they walked, the more he doubted his abilities. Good soldiers had fallen that shouldn't have, soldiers who surpassed his experience. With their advanced technology and training, their forces should crush the resistance, not the other way around. How was this possible?

He and his men resumed their journey to the ridge. Once at the top, Kaytrix could make out the battlefield in the distance. Billows of smoke rose into the air from destroyed turrets, the ground littered with bodies and banners bearing the Archarian crest.

At the bottom of the ridge, a building stood cemented in the ground as a permanent structure with fortified walls. A man stood outside under the canopy with another soldier, gazing at a holo-screen. The rankings on his shoulders signified his position. It was Captain Wesk.

Kaytrix motioned his squad forward and they struggled down the sloppy terrain. At last, they reached the captain. Kaytrix inhaled, trying to calm his rising emotions. The walk across camp had drained his excitement, replacing it with dread. What had he led his men into?

"Lieutenant Torex reporting for duty, sir!" He saluted, eyeing the captain in his peripheral vision.

Captain Wesk dismissed the soldier beside him. He looked exhausted. Mud smeared his uniform and crusted his face. The bags under his eyes hinted at a lack of sleep, but hope glimmered in his eyes.

The rain pelted Kaytrix's face relentlessly as he waited for the captain to speak.

"Lieutenant Torex. The admiral mentioned sending us reinforcements."

"We're ready to serve, Captain. Where shall we bunk?"

The captain's face contorted, his eyes wild. "Lieutenant, look around you."

Kaytrix looked around the camp. He'd seen enough on his way here, but the captain's question caught him off guard. What did he want him to see specifically?

"Sir?"

"Men don't live long enough to worry about their next meal, never mind where they will sleep. And if you make it a day, nightmares will rob you of rest," Captain Wesk said. The muscles in his neck tightened as he ground his teeth.

"Yes, sir! Admiral Ackon did not make us aware of your situation, sir!"

"Well, now you are aware. It's taking everything we can muster to fight this opponent. They pulled back their forces two rotations ago, allowing us to gain a stronger foothold and call for reinforcements, but I fear it won't last long. We need to hurry if we're going to stop them. I fear they are planning to leave the planet."

"Sir, if I may, what enemy are we fighting? The last I heard, there wasn't a force in the galaxy that could rival our power."

Wesk's body went rigid, his hand resting on his blaster as if that was its normal position. "Look, Lieutenant, it's above my authority to share the details, let alone with an officer of your nature. But you might not make it out of here alive, so listen. Don't underestimate the enemy. They're quick, smart, and vicious. If given the chance, they would kill all of us in a heartbeat. We must do everything to keep their kind on this planet. If we don't, they will ravage the galaxy. Everything we know is at risk."

Kaytrix's skin crawled. Did he imagine what the captain said? Were they really fighting an enemy that matched, if not surpassed, their might? Images of his ma and father surfaced. He couldn't let the enemy jeopardize all he loved and worked for. He would do everything in his power to keep the enemy from leaving.

Kaytrix focused on the captain, about to ask a question, when a loud roar distracted him. The new sound seemed familiar from battle simulations he trained in, but the enormity of the sound shook him to his core. A large striking dropship with pulsating blue engines flew overhead and prepared to land on the outskirts of the camp.

Once landed on the marsh terrain, the dropship's cargo hold opened. Several platoons emerged from the ship and approached the camp, their movement a chorus of rhythmic marching.

Kaytrix couldn't guess how many soldiers there were, but they appeared fierce.

"Perfect." Captain Wesk nodded. "More reinforcements." He glanced back at Kaytrix. "Lieutenant, your squad will join these platoons on the front lines with Commander Dest. I'll send you the coordinates to your post. Commander Dest will bring you up to speed on what strategies we will use to defeat the enemy."

Kaytrix saluted. "Thank you, sir."

He turned away, and his gauntlet beeped. Information displayed in a hologram above his wrist. He pressed the screen to view the coordinates Captain Wesk sent. A marker pulsed on a map, showing the coordinates of the battlefield. The calculations on his screen determined it was a short trek to reach it.

He noted the open field flanked by high rocky terrain surrounded by trees with a deep crevasse near the opposite end of the field. Beside it, a red marker pulsed as information scrolled across his display. It was where the enemy kept their ships.

"This way, men." He motioned with his hand to move out.

His squad was quiet as they journeyed to the battlefield, their normal banter silenced by the disturbed thoughts they were all sharing. The other platoons joined them, their sloshing feet carving their silence, and their trail, deeper.

Kaytrix walked carefully as the mud turned into rocky terrain. The rain chilled him, soaking through his cape and through parts of armored skin. He missed the heat of Drenna, as odd as that was to admit. But it was more than Drenna; it was the idea that they were invincible that he missed.

"Lieutenant! Take cover!" A voice said as they rounded the trees and faced the clearing of the battlefield.

Kaytrix peered against the darkening sky to see a man shielded behind a wall of rock, waving his arms frantically.

Then a bone chilling sound. A pop followed by a loud roar.

"Down!" Kaytrix yelled, falling face-first onto the rocky terrain. His men scattered behind him, their armor hitting stone as they dropped.

The missile flew overhead and exploded against the rockface. It shook the ground beneath them and disturbed the mountain.

He got to his feet. Large turrets from their side fired multiple rockets at the opposing treeline, creating craters of dirt and debris. A loud roar tore above them—another counterstrike from the enemy. It arced over the peak of the mountain and disappeared on the other side.

"Are you trying to get yourself killed?" a voice called, irritated.

Kaytrix glanced to the soldier's rankings on his shoulders. Charred metal was all that remained.

"Get behind a rock, you twit!"

The platoons moved from behind him and into the various trenches. Kaytrix motioned his men to do the same and neared the commander's side. Several of their turrets still operated, while others sparked and smoked, destroyed. The battlefield looked worse than from the top of the ridge. Before them, fallen Archarians soldiers scattered the ground.

"Commander Dest?"

"Who else? Gee, are we that desperate they are sending greenhorns? The enemy almost killed you just now!" he said with a shake of his head.

"How long have you been fighting under these conditions, Commander?" Kaytrix called over another roar, ignoring his comment. He glimpsed a fortified bunker with an enemy gun standing as an impenetrable mountain.

"Too long!" Commander Dest answered. "Your arrival got them excited. Woo, look at these reinforcements." His gaze settled on something behind him.

Kaytrix glanced over his shoulder to see more platoons approaching and taking cover in the trenches. Their respective commanders convened on his position, acknowledging Commander Dest.

"Is there just the one turret?" Only one dominated the field, but there could be another hiding farther in the forest.

"It only takes one! That turret has been laying waste to my men for longer than I care to admit," Commander Dest fumed. "We need to destroy it so we can press the enemy back and destroy their grounded ships."

Kaytrix nodded. "Could we use an aerial attack to destroy them?"

Commander Dest wiped his running nose with the back of his hand. "No. We can't penetrate their shielding. We have been successful with some hand-to-hand, but they're so damn strong it takes ten of our soldiers to their one!"

The turret had ceased fire and a lone figure stood before it, its tattered cloak billowing in the wind.

"That's one of them?" Kaytrix asked. The soldier stood taller and broader than anyone he'd ever seen.

"Yes." Commander Dest scoffed. "It's like a bloody robot. Doesn't eat, sleep, or seem to tire. It just stands there and murders."

Kaytrix's spine tingled. "One soldier did all this?"

"Well, there was a handful to begin with, but that's the last one. At least, I hope. The only thing that works on those bastards is our blades."

Kaytrix studied the mysterious alien on the field. He couldn't see any detail past the tattered cloak it wore.

"The only way we're going to destroy that turret and destroy their ships is a diversion." The commander pulled charges out of a carryon. "The platoons will distract the turret while another, smaller group gets close enough to stuff these down that sucker's throat."

"I'll go," Kaytrix offered. "My men and I will get the job done."

The commander hesitated.

Kaytrix feared he held the same grudge against him as the other commanding officers.

"I like your bravery, Lieutenant. Alright, you and your men can go. Just don't screw this up," Commander Dest said. He grinned, but his eyes betrayed the fact that he'd seen men die because of that turret. Did he expect Kaytrix to die as well? Kaytrix would do his best, as he'd always done.

"Wreak hell on them," Kaytrix said as he took the charges, his hands shaking. "Alright, men, we're heading out through that bush line to deliver the explosives," he called over another missile. He regrouped with his squad and waited.

"Onward to glory!" Commander Dest yelled when he and the platoons charged the battlefield.

The turret began firing and the alien soldier lunged forward.

Kaytrix and his squad bolted for the trees, Ryll and Duke taking point. It was just as they practiced in the academy, only now it was the real thing. Were his men afraid?

Just as they set off, the remaining platoons emerged from the trenches and stormed the battlefield. The enemy turret whirled on them and launched its vicious assault. A deep pulsing sound emanated from its barrel as it attacked. Its strength tore through the first line of men, decimating them.

Kaytrix's heart ached. Never had he witnessed such brutality. Fresh bodies already lay scattered across the battlefield. As more soldiers charged, they were shot down. He pushed past his feelings and hurried through the bush, avoiding branches while racing against time. If he could hear the turret firing, he had a chance.

He'd only seen a fraction of this enemy's power. What Captain Wesk said was true: if they left this planet, the enemy would destroy everything he loved, including his parents. He couldn't let that happen. If he ever wanted to do something that mattered, the time was now, even if it meant losing his life.

Suddenly, the turret turned its attention on them and opened fire. Rapid blasts of hot plasma shot in their direction. Kaytrix dropped to the ground, hitting hard. The rounds raked the bush, melting branches and disturbing the soil. After completing a round, the turret resumed fire on the battlefield.

Through the smoke of the attack, Kaytrix glimpsed the platoons charging the turret. They closed in, able to evade further fire, but their numbers were few. They took cover in trenches and behind debris, launching grenades at the turret's opening and at the lone soldier.

"Let's move it!" he called to his men as he rose to his feet.

His squad charged ahead as he regained his footing and darted through the bush. They paused behind a mound of disheveled dirt to ready the charges.

"Hurry!" Ryll panted.

Kaytrix's hands fumbled. Shouts and wails of pain intensified as he readied the final grenade. They were in position to charge the base of the fortified structure, but it was still a fair distance away. They needed to get closer.

Kaytrix summoned his courage and readied to launch himself at the base of the turret. He was ready to attack when the turret ceased fire. The tapping of rain drove the silence of the battlefield deep into his memory and a wave of dread washed through him.

He was too late.

A soul-scratching screech penetrated the silence, sending a chill through his soul. He peered at the battlefield. There lay the platoons strewn across the open range, and triumphantly above them stood the lone black-robed figure.

"Lieutenant, we can still take out the turret," Duke whispered from behind him.

"Agreed. When I say, we will charge the turret and throw the grenades inside." He hoped they could get that far without dying, and quicker still, to escape the blast.

Duke and Ryll nodded and waited. They lay silent in the wet grass, their armor absorbing moisture. The turret turned but did not fire as it sought new targets. He waited until the turret faced the other way.

"Now!" he ordered.

They started their approach at a run, emerging from the bush as a wild wind. The turret repositioned itself, turning its barrel toward him and his men. His heart tightened in his chest, the air he breathed choked him. They were halfway there.

A few more meters.

Ten more steps.

The barrel released a slew of green energy.

Kaytrix ducked, missing the attack, but a dark shadow raced to meet them. The grenades in his hands were heavier than before, his legs numb. He might not make it.

"Keep going!" Duke yelled from behind.

"You're almost there!" Ryll said.

Then it happened. A terrified scream erupted behind him followed by blaster shots and more screams. The horrible sound of sharp metal meeting armor scratched his ears and his confidence.

He turned to see his men being massacred. His squad, the tough, pushy, mouthy men who bothered him nonstop, had given their lives for the mission, for him. He couldn't let his men die in vain—he had to complete his mission.

He stumbled over the terrain until he reached the turret. He grasped the grenades and scaled the stones on the side of the bunker. The turret turned toward him; a loud humming shook his resolve. It aimed at him as he grasped the embrasure's ledge and launched the grenades deep inside the bunker. He leapt for cover behind a pile of rocks and squeezed the detonator.

A furious blast tore through the embrasure of the fortified hold. Rock and debris fell in chunks around him, the smaller pebbles deflecting off his armor. His ears rang, and disorientation took over. He uncovered his head as the last of the debris finished crumbling around him, and he peered over his refuge.

Smoke billowed from the top of the destroyed bunker as the driving rain pinched his face. Across the battlefield, many soldiers lay fallen, lost in the confrontation. He was the only survivor.

Fear consumed him as he stood and readied his weapon. A powerful adversary such as this posed a tremendous threat not only to Archaria, but to the entire Dexsortes galaxy. He couldn't fathom what atrocities this enemy could commit if they left the planet.

Kaytrix activated his comm to report to Captain Wesk. It was imperative they move the remaining platoons in and destroy the grounded ships. He was about to speak, when an eerie sensation crept up his spine. He spun to see the robed soldier emerging from the cloud of dust, its eyes glowing a vibrant and eerie green. The cloak it wore fell away in a blast of wind, revealing the robotic skeletal frame of his enemy.

Kaytrix fired his weapon, but a shimmering green rippled over the figure's body. The soldier had a shield. He remembered what Commander Dest had said about their blades and hand-to-hand combat, but he was alone. Could he face such a powerful foe, one with the strength of ten men?

Closer now, the enemy took a swing at him with its massive robotic arm. Sharp protruding claws threatened to tear his face as it struck. He stepped backward, narrowly escaping the attack.

He dodged another strike, his adrenaline surging to a new height as he prepared to fire his rifle again. The black-armored opponent closed in, evading his attack and kicking his weapon from his hand.

Kaytrix snatched his sidearm and fired off a round in desperation. The energy hit its target but rolled off his rival's armor. Before he could reload his clip, the enemy's robotic hand grasped his weapon and crushed it. With its other hand, it grabbed him by the throat and lifted him into the air.

Kaytrix desperately pried at the sharp, dagger-like fingers, but his strength was not enough. He choked and sputtered as the neon green eyes beneath the metal armor glowered at him. Mercy could not exist in a being with eyes as cold and callous as this. Was this how he was going to die?

Then he remembered his blade sheathed on his hip. He summoned the last of his failing concentration to complete the simple task of reaching for it. His muscles refusing the motion as if weighed down. His temples throbbed as the killing pressure increased.

Kaytrix gasped, frantically trying to draw in another breath. He struggled to loosen the blade from its sheath as he fumbled frantically, frustration thwarting his attempts.

At last, it came free. This was his only chance to survive. It was imperative he complete his mission. He took a blind swing with the last of his energy. To his surprise, the blade met slight resistance before plunging deeper.

Kaytrix opened his eyes as the tight grasp around his neck loosened. He gasped, able to breathe again. The blade protruded out of the creature's right eye. No doubt he'd injured its brain. A fluke of luck.

The enemy released him, dropping him to the ground. His knees snapped and buckled from the height of the drop. He cradled his knees. They felt broken, but he didn't have time to worry about that now. He didn't know if this mysterious enemy still posed a threat, and he wasn't about to take any chances.

The soldier towered above him, staggering from side to side. It's outstretched hand that once held him, frozen in its position. The body leaned forward. It was going to crush him. Kaytrix struggled to stand, his knees shooting pain into his legs as he stood. He managed two steps and struggled to take another.

A slow and angry hiss reverberated between the mouth plates of the alien, sending a chill through him. He turned as its stance weakened. With a sudden clash, the titan of metal crumbled to its knees. The soldier kneeled an arm's length away. A hot, slow breath forced itself through the fanged grates of its armored face, as if trying to utter one last threat. Its remaining eye flashed a wicked green when it grew dull and darkened with death. The soldiers' lifeless body then collapsed to the side with a crushing groan.

Kaytrix gasped a sigh of relief, but this battle was far from over. Two ships remained, harboring countless more soldiers. They had to be stopped before they escaped into the galaxy and wreaked havoc on innocent worlds. If the Archarian soldiers couldn't stand against this opponent, the alliance was in trouble.

He called the captain again, activating his comm with a tap.

"Lieutenant, what's your status?" the captain's voice echoed.

Kaytrix struggled to speak, a harsh rasp escaping his body. He clutched his throat. The soldier damaged it in the fight.

"Lieutenant, come in? What's your status?" Captain Wesk's voice echoed again.

A gust of wind hit him from behind and threw him onto his stomach. A deafening roar enveloped his ears. The wind intensified, whipping through the field.

"Lieutenant! Report!" Captain Wesk said through the comm in his ear, his voice faint.

Kaytrix turned over. Again, he tried answering his captain, yelling as loud as he could, but the same raspy sound came out.

Out of the field before him, the enemy ships rose into the sky. His stomach churned as green weapons' fire descended through the clouds and struck the camp. Emptiness consumed him as flame surpassed the treetops. The ships finished with their destructive mission in a matter of moments and slipped into the clouds and out of view.

He had failed.

Chapter 3
THE COUNCIL

Kaytrix stumbled through the arkross and fell onto the floor of the Grand Tower, his boots and body slathered with the mud of O'ber. He had walked back most of the way, but his knees had given out at some point. Or was it his heart?

The imperial guards rushed to his side. "What happened, Lieutenant?" one asked him.

Kaytrix indicated to them he couldn't speak, using his hands to explain his voicelessness.

"Call for a medic!" one shouted to the other.

Out of his peripheral vision, one guard activated his comm. The other guard hoisted him to his feet. Soon the medics were entering the arkross chambers with a medical bed behind them.

"Help me get him onto the bed," a medic said.

The guards helped the medics lay him on a stretcher. "Don't worry, Lieutenant, we will find out what happened from the command center," one guard said.

Kaytrix caught the guard by the arm and squeezed. The guard appeared confused and Kaytrix pointed to his satchel, which was dripping in mud. The guard nodded, understanding his silent gesture, and opened it to reveal his blade.

"Give me a holo-screen!" the guard demanded.

At first, Kaytrix hesitated, not wanting to relive the battle, but the medics were talking. With the damage done to his knees and throat, he would be in hyperbaric healing for several days. He couldn't wait that long for the admiral to hear his report.

The medics squabbled while he typed on the holo-screen. He focused harder to ignore their voices. They wanted to rush him along, but the guard answered with a tone that ended their persistence.

He composed the report and lay back on the stretcher. He glimpsed the imperial guard leave at a run. As he tried to prepare for what would happen next, he got lost in his view of the ceiling passing above him.

Soon he was in the medical bay. The doctors removed his armor and sliced him free of his under-armor. The medical crew gently placed him in the hyperbaric chamber. A nurse attached monitoring devices to his chest and his temple. Her chilly hands reminded him of the torrential rains on O'ber.

He flinched as memories surfaced from the battle. Soldiers falling, his squad dying, and the haunting green eyes emerging from the dust . . .

"Activating the chamber," a voice said.

Someone slipped a respirator over his nose and mouth, and he lost consciousness.

Kaytrix woke to a massive headache. Thirst trapped his tongue to the roof of his mouth, and a strange sensation tingled throughout his body. Was it exhaustion or renewed muscles?

Frigid air breathed on his exposed feet and hands, annoying him. He was out of the hyperbaric chamber and laid on a stretcher. What he wouldn't give for the heat of Drenna.

He opened his eyes to a dull gray room. Holographic charts hung around the room displayed his medical information, one focused on his throat.

He tried to look around, but found himself held firmly in place. A machine with sophisticated medical lasers locked around his neck, working to repair his damaged larynx.

A sudden surge of guilt for surviving welled up inside him. The moment before his men fell replayed in his mind, plaguing him. If only he had targeted the enemy soldier first, then his squad would still be alive. And that soldier . . . something about the way their technology surpassed the Archarians' disturbed him. In fact, it made him feel an unfamiliar emotion: fear.

He hoped an analysis of the blade could help them discover a better way to fight this enemy. Facing an opponent armed only with a blade wasn't something he wanted to experience again.

He closed his eyes.

How did the admiral take his report? His detailed fight with the enemy was sure to catch the admiral's attention.

His hands started to sweat and his stomach knotted as apprehension gripped him. To see the admiral face-to-face and give his report in person would prove difficult. How the mission had ended was his responsibility. Could the admiral forgive his incompetence and assign him a new squad? He hoped by the time the machine finished, he'd have the courage to retell the event and to answer questions the admiral might have.

He continued to lie still. He took in a sharp breath, trying to release his festering anxiety. He needed a distraction. How was his ma doing with her new medicine? Had his father found time to rest?

Time passed and the lasers working to repair his throat stopped. The machine powered down and the collar directing the healing retracted from around his neck. At last, the procedure was complete.

Kaytrix hesitated to speak, partly fearful the machine had failed, but also afraid to break the silence he'd created since returning from the battlefield.

A nurse entered the room, startling him. She checked the machine's status and inputted information onto her holo-screen.

She glanced at him. "Lieutenant Torex. How are you feeling?"

He hesitated. The question forced him to respond. "As well as any soldier could be." His voice sounded normal. Not the raspy one he remembered trying to warn Captain Wesk. The wonders of Archarian medicine.

She appeared impartial to his hesitance to answer, noting everything in her file.

"How long was I in the hyperbaric chamber?" he asked.

"Three rotations," she replied. She examined his throat, her icy hands gliding over where the machine worked. "There are no signs of bruising or extensive damage. Scans show the healing is complete. Please dress and report to the council."

Kaytrix sat up from the bed. "The council?"

The nurse turned to look back at him, seeming to note his half-exposed body before answering, "That's right. The councillors wish to speak to you."

Kaytrix nodded as he slipped the sheer material off the rest of his body and dressed in a fresh layer of clothes and his armor.

It was best he spoke to the council first. At this time, he wasn't sure he could take more poking and prodding from the Warrior clan and their entitled position of power. If he could satisfy the council with his efforts, then he could continue to serve. At least, he hoped.

Kaytrix walked into the lift and selected his destination. His optimism soured into nerves. He had no reason to be nervous, and yet an inescapable heat rose throughout his body.

The lift came to a stop. He drew in a quick breath, his heart beating fast. He had never met the councillors before. Sure, he'd seen them in a prerecording of congratulations at his graduation ceremony and in their daily media, but it was not the same as meeting them in person. They embodied the purest of Archarian qualities; that's why the people chose them to represent the three clans. To be in their presence was to be in the company of wisdom.

The lift opened and he stepped out. Another similar hallway greeted him, but to his right stood two large wooden doors. This was the only level to possess doors such as these. He approached the entrance, acknowledging the guards standing on either side.

When he reached the door, he grasped the handle but hesitated to go inside. With a calming inhale, he used his training to rid his mind of any distractions.

Focus.

He breathed out.

He was grateful the Warrior clans trained all their soldiers in this mind-calming technique. It allowed the body to regain stability and the soldier to regain focus and control on their mission.

He pushed the door open and entered.

The room greeted him with a brilliant brightness of whites and grays. An arched ceiling rose above him, taller than several men. At the end of this short room, great windows from floor to ceiling allowed light to cascade in, and to the right was another archway. He walked the short distance to the doorway and entered the inner chambers.

The main room was an even larger room shaped like a key. He observed the long hallway he stood in. Imperial guards stood on either side below Archarian banners. Vast statues of heroes in expressive poses exalted either wall in rows, their perfection immortalized in stone. They prompted respect for the Archarian civilization's beginning millennia ago.

A sweet-smelling scent wafted toward him. The aroma from the burning candles reminded him of trees in bloom at the farm during the warm season. His mind relaxed, but his memories of the farm and simpler times faded as he drew near the end of the passage.

Before him the primary gathering place of the council, a large crescent-shaped table in the middle of the round room. He could hear the quiet mutterings of the council and others seated with them, the allied members of their alliance.

He identified the council members: Karva Norda represented the Farmer clan, Perseph the Warrior clan, and Sarneft the Creative clan. The others seated with them he recognized as their allies, various other races from powerful worlds. They ranged in humanoid likeness to creatures with fur and beings of pure energy for bodies.

Only the council and admirals ever spoke or met their allies, simply because it was impossible for every Archarian to be acquainted with them.

It appeared their meeting ended as the allied members rose from the table, bowed to the council, and left the room. They walked past him on their way out, and a wave of awe swelled in his heart. It was surreal to see them in person.

"Lieutenant Torex," a voice called.

He turned to see the council waiting for him. His heart sped. He wasn't prepared to give his report. The echo of his footsteps drew the others' attention to his approach.

"Councillors." He saluted. "I am reporting as instructed."

"Lieutenant Torex, yes. Please, join us," requested Karva Norda, gesturing to the center of the crescent table.

Kaytrix stood in its center and waited. The three members sat at the widest of the crescent, farthest from the opening. They dressed in robes of the finest material, embellished with golden embroidered trim and the colors of their clan: red for Warrior, blue for Creative, and black for Farmer. Their wrists bore gauntlets of the highest grade, capable of multiple functions. Atop their heads they dawned delicate crowns of silver, accented with communication and holographic display abilities.

Standing in the middle of the table made Kaytrix feel as if he was on trial. He closed his eyes to relax.

"Something wrong?" a scrutinizing voice asked.

Alarmed at the woman's tone, he opened his eyes and fixed his gaze on the individuals before him.

The council member Sarneft popped a delicate fruit into her mouth as she analyzed him. Her blue Creative clan marking shone brightly on the side of her face compared to her pale skin.

"Pardon me, councillor. My nerves are getting the best of me." He observed the others.

"It is an honor to meet you, Lieutenant," Karva said, his tone sincere. "The admiral made us aware of your last mission and the heroic demonstration of courage you displayed on the battlefield of O'ber."

Kaytrix nodded. He wasn't sure what he did was so courageous. It was a mission to complete and merely self-defense against the enemy.

"We want to talk about your experience. That is, if you can," spoke Perseph. He sat with his arms crossed, his eyes narrow.

Perseph was thin, his eye sockets shallow and purple with age. A scraggly beard gathered at his chin. He reminded Kaytrix of a farm rodent, sickly and skinny no matter how much it ate.

"I am able," he said.

"Please begin when you are ready," Karva spoke.

Kaytrix shared his story. Saying it aloud proved harder than he anticipated, the sights and sounds returning to haunt his memory. The evil glare of death and the callous hatred from his enemy were enough to shake him to the core.

"Is there anything else you experienced? Anything that may benefit our knowledge of this enemy?" Karva asked.

Memories of being strangled resurfaced. "The enemy's shields are impenetrable with energy-based weapons. Commander Dest informed me only our blades appear to work."

The council members glanced at each other.

"Sounds like they have gotten stronger," Perseph commented. "It's interesting to me that you are the only one who survived your mission, Lieutenant."

"Agreed," Sarneft said. "Is there something else you want to share?" she asked, raising an eyebrow at him.

"Pardon?" he asked.

"Did you fight, Lieutenant? We lost experienced commanders and yet only you returned," Perseph said.

Kaytrix wrestled with his rising anger. "I told you everything exactly as it happened, councillor. The ships that left the planet possess an alarming power, one that rivals our own. I stand before you today because Archaria needs to know everything they can to protect the alliance. It would honor me to continue this fight. Once we involve the allies, we—"

"You needn't worry about that, Lieutenant," Perseph said. "We will handle those details."

"Forgive me, councillor." Kaytrix folded his arms behind his back and waited. He regretted allowing himself to show too much enthusiasm.

Karva leaned back in his chair, eyeing him. "I am curious, Lieutenant. Why, after all this, do you want to keep fighting?"

"There is nothing else that I want to do, sir. Serving Archaria is my purpose."

There was a pause in the room.

"What do we think?" Sarneft asked, peering toward the other members. "He'd make an excellent candidate for our project."

Perseph and Karva exchanged glances.

"We've been down this road, let's not repeat history." Perseph scowled.

"There is no better candidate," Sarneft stated. She crossed her arms and stared at Perseph until he lowered his gaze and crossed his arms.

"Then that settles it." Karva said, standing.

What did they mean? He found it difficult to understand their broken speech between themselves.

Karva beamed at him. "We have a proposition for you that aligns well with your wish to continue your service to Archaria."

"Councillor?"

"We want to promote you to commander and assign you a new mission commanding a starship."

Kaytrix couldn't believe what he was hearing. He had always wanted to command his own starship, but this wasn't the way he envisioned his promotion happening. Skipping a rank smacked of desperation. It was wrong. It took solar rotations for someone to earn the rank of commander. He could only imagine what kind of treatment he would get from his peers if they learned of this.

"I don't think I qualify, councillor. I have only served ten solar rotations in the Warrior clan."

"Of course, you qualify," Karva argued. "I've assessed your file, Lieutenant Torex. You graduated with honors, aced all your classes and training modules, displayed aptitude in all the starship command scenarios. Led a squad of soldiers for five solar rotations. The courage you displayed on O'ber and your experience fighting this new enemy will benefit the alliance. In fact, we have already promoted you." Karva said.

Kaytrix accessed the records on his gauntlet in disbelief. To his surprise, his public profile now read as "Commander Kaytrix Torex."

"No ceremony?" he asked. Commanding a starship was an impressive feat usually celebrated.

"No time." Perseph scowled at him. "You were in the hyperbaric chamber when we could have performed the ceremony."

Perseph's words robbed him of the recognition he sought, but it was too late to change his mind. He wanted to protect the alliance and his parents from ever experiencing the destruction he had witnessed on O'ber, and if this was how he had to do it, then so be it.

"Very well, I will command your starship. What is my mission?"

"Report to Admiral Ackon. He will have the details for you," Sarneft instructed. "That will be everything, Commander Torex."

Hearing his new title spoken shocked him. He saluted, turned, and left their presence. As he exited the chambers, a cloud shrouded his mind. The entire experience wasn't what he expected, and neither were the councillors as the media portrayed them. Sarneft was snarky, not loving and creative. Perseph was sly and deceptive, not courageous and honorable. Even Karva Norda was desperate, not resourceful.

He struggled with their hostility and the surprise of his sudden promotion. Why was he promoted before they asked him? How did they know he would say yes? The council also appeared unaffected by the devastation wreaked upon the camp, as if it was only a setback. Shouldn't they be more concerned? And why hadn't the allies been involved? The guidelines of the alliance stated they helped other members in times of difficulty. Their support on the battlefield could have changed the outcome of the entire mission, even if only one member of the alliance aided them.

He thought of the Varanus' might for a moment and their raging power. Their strength and agility alone would have prevented so many casualties. The lizard species were adept with hand-to-hand combat and armed with talons and claws. They would have torn through the enemy's shields and ripped them apart. So why had they not been called?

Kaytrix rode the lift to the command center. He squeezed his eyes shut. A lot had happened in the last few rotations, and dwelling on something he couldn't control wasn't going to help him focus on his new mission. Regardless of the council and their decisions, he needed to put the battle behind him.

He entered the command center and a distinct feeling struck him. The same unease as before filled the room like an invisible forcefield, and the discomfort showed on the men's faces. Admirals and soldiers stared at holo-screens, muttering, pointing, shaking their heads, and pointing to other parts of the display.

He identified several fleets and the planets they patrolled. He viewed the displayed tactical data and recognized ships that were on high alert while others remained on standby.

Kaytrix searched the room for the admiral. He stood with two other vice admirals, their faces contorted with furrowed brows and scowls as they chatted.

He swallowed, a pit forming in his stomach. Seeing the admirals concerned was not a good sign. He made eye contact with them and waited.

Admiral Ackon motioned him to join.

He drew near and saluted. "Sir," he greeted, his eyes following the departing vice admirals.

"Congratulations on your promotion," Ackon said, his tone dry as he touched the display controls.

"Thank you, sir." A blue holographic display lit before Kaytrix. The holo-screen flashed, and different information appeared. He recognized the star system.

"The Zaguarz?" The holo-projection of the planet displayed the details of the species. He remembered learning of them in his studies. They were one of Archaria's oldest allies. They were tall, noble creatures ruled by a chieftain, their hunting and agricultural skills highly sought after throughout the galaxy. In fact, the Farmer clan learned a lot from the Zaguarz when it came to planting and harvesting.

"Correct, Lieu—Commander Torex," Admiral Ackon replied.

"What awaits us there?" Kaytrix stared through the holo-screen at the admiral. Whatever worried him, he kept it hidden.

"There's been a disturbance reported by the Zaguarz. One of their valueable merchant ships has gone missing after a brutal attack. We've tried to communicate with the Zaguarz since then, but there's been no response. We suspect their arkross is offline or damaged. You are to command the starship *Ro'arck* and investigate with the *R'nalz* and *Tezner*. Find out their status and if the incident relates to O'ber."

Kaytrix nodded. It made sense. The Zaguarz planet was not too far from the outer rim, and in this case, O'ber.

"Thank you. We will leave immediately. Sir, if I can ask something?" Kaytrix said, pausing.

"Yes, Commander Torex?"

"What happened to the fleet above O'ber? Were they not successful in stopping the ships from leaving?"

The admiral's face fell. "No, Commander. That is why we are sending our elite starships on this mission. We can't afford to lose forces like that again. That is everything for now, Commander. Board the *Narvent* station and talk to the lead operator. He will have your ship ready."

Kaytrix saluted and left the room. As he approached the arkross, he wasn't sure what he should be feeling. He was excited about commanding his own starship, but also concerned with the councillors' behavior, and now this issue with the Zaguarz.

He breathed in. *Focus.*

He needed the strength of clarity, but despite his affirmations, focus eluded him.

Chapter 4

CLASH

Kaytrix stood before the arkross, watching it light up as it dialed in coordinates for the *Narvent* station. He fidgeted with his cape clasp. Commanding a starship so soon in his military career was sure to turn heads, but the council made it clear that they needed his experience with the enemy. Besides, he'd earned it, hadn't he? After putting up with the slurs and insults from his superiors.

He sighed. The markings on his skin shouldn't matter and neither should titles. He had a job to do, and the council had chosen him to do it. He forced his breath out. This mission wasn't the training modules he'd aced; it was real with life-and-death consequences.

He stepped through the activated portal and boarded the *Narvent*. Like in the Great Tower, a round secure room contained the arkross. Bulkheads and panels of steel surrounded him, lit by several glowing orbs of white light that strobed softly.

The air was frigid. He rubbed his hands together when several imperial guards entered through the doorway with a woman. A quick once-over of her standard-issue jumpsuit informed him she ranked as the lead operator's assistant. Her shoulders bore the insignia of the station: a circle within a circle. On the side of her face glowed hues of radiant blue, the identifying symbols of the Creative clan.

The woman spoke first, her voice a musical wind chime. "Greetings, Commander Torex. I am Karrin. We've been expecting you." She smiled.

"Nice to meet you, Karrin," Kaytrix said. "I was told the *Ro'arck* is ready for departure?"

"Yes, Commander," Karrin answered. "Right this way, please."

Sliding doors parted in front of them and he followed Karrin into the next section of the station, a long gray corridor lit with narrow lights beneath the walkway and along the ceiling. Every so many paces, the walkway diverted off the main path and ended at a closed door. He only remembered certain aspects of the station from his studies, such as the different docking ports. The finer details of the station's operations weren't included in his training. It was a complex station riddled with various access ports, stairways, and lifts that connected to each other.

At the end of the corridor stood another door and Karrin accessed it with a code. Through this door was another larger corridor. Vast windows framed one side, allowing him to see the great arms of the station encircling the command dome.

He noted the refueling canisters below specific docking ports, and the specific markings above each port. Red for fuel, gray for supplies, and white for repairs. Everything the station could do to sustain the coming and going of starships was remarkable.

They entered a lift and a holographic map displayed before them. A kind robotic voice asked for a destination to which Karrin selected the command dome. There was a slight jolt as the lift moved, then the doors parted to another level. The transportation was instantaneous.

Before them was the command dome of the station. A command deck floated at its center surrounded by an orb of glass. Through it hung the massive arms of the station, and various ships searched for ports among ships already docked. This ideal view allowed the lead operator to observe everything around the station.

The lead operator stood in center of the control deck with his hands behind his back. He monitored multiple holo-screens at once, giving orders to those seated around him. Occasionally he touched the side of his head, activating and ending communications to various channels. In the security footage stood Kaytrix's image and in the next panel over, the image of the arkross. Truly, he saw everything.

"Come," Karrin said, startling him. "He's ready to meet you."

The man turned to face him. "Commander," he greeted. "Welcome aboard the *Narvent*. I am the lead operator of this station, but you can call me Zilas," Zilas said, saluting.

Kaytrix noted the Creative clan marking on his face and returned the salute. "Nice to meet you."

Zilas appeared younger than most men—youthful even. Kaytrix could only speculate his age, for Archarians aged well and lived longer than most humanoid races. He himself was young compared to those higher in society such as the councillors and admiral who'd been serving Archaria for several generations.

Zilas's eyes sparkled. "You will command one of the finest starships our fleet has ever known. The first of their kind," he said as he activated a holo-screen of specs.

Kaytrix marveled at the intricate light that outlined his soon-to-be starship. Her design unlike any other ship he studied.

"The *Ro'arck* and her sister ships possess an increased flight speed and shield durability, with heavier hull armor and turrets. Their unique design allows for quick navigation correction."

Kaytrix nodded, impressed. Gazing upon the sleek design excited him. He studied the machine he was going to command. Destruction masked as a work of art.

"Commanding her will be the same as what you learned in basic training," Zilas said. "They have the same systems, but function faster. Now, if you are ready, Karrin will escort you to the *Ro'arck*."

Kaytrix saluted. "Thank you. Wish us luck out there."

Zilas returned the salute. "You don't need luck, you have the *Ro'arck*!" he said as he returned to his post.

Kaytrix half smiled, amused. Zilas's enthusiasm was infectious and, for a moment, any doubt of facing the enemy vanished. Confidence budded in his heart as he looked at the *Ro'arck* again. With this kind of starship, he was certain he could face anything.

Karrin showed him to the lift and selected one of the right arms of the station as their destination. When they stepped out, another open corridor framed by windows lay before them. She led him to a closed hatch and entered a code into the control panel.

"Take this access corridor and follow it all the way to the end. The *Ro'arck* is docked there. Peace to Archaria, Commander," she said in farewell.

"Peace to Archaria," he said, entering the passageway that connected the ship and station together.

A solemn path of gray lay before him. Blinking white lights lit his way to the docked ship while large panes of thick glass domed the walkway. Archaria hung in the distance and the majesty of the *Ro'arck* struck him as she floated in her port.

He approached the *Ro'arck's* access panel, his footsteps a dull echo along the quiet access corridor. Once he reached the end, he touched the display and the doors withdrew from each other, revealing a small room with another set of doors. He stepped inside. A green light indicated the chamber was pressurized and the doors before him opened to reveal a young man saluting.

"Commander Torex, I am Lieutenant Levro, sir," he greeted. He held his youthful face in a blank gaze.

"Lieutenant." Kaytrix saluted. "Nice to meet you. Are we ready to embark?"

"Yes, sir," Levro replied. "I have debriefed everyone on the situation. Your report was a great resource for us, sir."

"I'm glad to hear that, Lieutenant. I look forward to meeting the bridge crew."

They entered a lift and selected the bridge as their destination. Levro teetered on the heels of his boots and Kaytrix glanced sideways at him. Levro held his arms behind his back, his gaze locked on the progression of the lift as he bit his bottom lip.

"You don't have to be nervous around me, Lieutenant. I was in your position not that long ago." *Literally*. His promotion was swift, and he was still adjusting to the sound and feel of being *Commander* Torex.

"Yes, sir." Levro said, his eyes bright.

Kaytrix recognized the same enthusiasm in Levro that he had, but also the same naivety. While Levro showed promise as a brilliant soldier, he still had much to learn.

The lift came to a stop with a gentle forward motion and the doors slid apart. Kaytrix entered the bridge and the aesthetic of colors and lights once again caught him off guard. The *Ro'arck* was, indeed, a piece of art. After a moment, his gaze left the contours of the ship and rested on the crew. His crew.

The faces of his squad members flashed before his eyes, and he composed himself. He had to do better this time.

"Greetings to you all. I am Commander Kaytrix Torex. Please announce your rank and name. Then we will begin our mission."

A burly brunette stood from her post on his right, a Creative clan symbol blazing on her face. "Analyst Officer Kersa reporting, sir." She saluted.

Another woman with a Creative clan marking stood. She was short with dirty blond hair. "Communications Officer Satki reporting."

"Weapons Officer Zenro reporting, sir," spoke a husky-voiced man from his left, the red symbol of the Warrior clan a contrast to his dark skin.

In front of him, a thinner man with a Creative clan symbol said, "Navigations Officer Auss reporting."

A man on his close left stood. His Creative clan marking matched his blue eyes. "Tech Specialist Tuce, reporting, sir."

Kaytrix saluted, acknowledging his crew. "It is a privilege to work alongside each of you. Let's get underway."

He approached the command chair with hesitation before resting in the seat. The moment was bittersweet. Finally, after solar rotations of arduous work, receiving constant opposition for his origin clan, his childhood dream of commanding a ship had come true. He only wished he'd earned it without losing his squad and skipping a rank.

"All systems are ready, Commander," Levro announced. "Sister ships *R'nalz* and *Tezner* are also ready to embark and aid us on our mission to Zaguarz." He stood on Kaytrix's left, viewing a holo-screen of all their systems.

"Acknowledged. Begin our departure," Kaytrix ordered.

The crew came alive. Each worked with an efficiency and fluid motion that he admired.

The *Ro'arck* detached from the *Narvent* and pulled away at a steady speed.

"We are out of range of the *Narvent*," Levro stated. "I have the coordinates for Zaguarz set. Sister ships confirm they are awaiting to embark on your order."

"Very well. Engage the hyperspace jump," Kaytrix said, watching in wonder as the portal for space travel opened before them. His first jump across space as a commander. The moment was surreal, but the jump signified things were getting real and dangerous. He suppressed any other distracting thoughts. It was time to be the soldier he had trained to be.

The *Ro'arck*, *Tezner*, and *R'nalz* exited their hyperspace jump and a sudden chill ran through Kaytrix. Zaguarz lay ahead, sheltered beneath planetary rings. The embrace of the rings could not hide her painful history. Even from this distance, her marred surface was apparent. Craters left divots all along her northern hemisphere. To the south, dark clouds collected, no doubt from the fires caused by the attack. The most disfiguring detail was the large gouge along the equator, as if they had dragged something heavy through the soft mantle for miles.

He rose from his seat, his hands clenched into fists as he approached the viewport. He couldn't see any ships, but their path of destruction was a clear sign they were here.

"Status report," he said.

"Nothing is appearing on the scanners except rock debris," responded Levro. "There are no signals from the surface either."

Kaytrix walked to the other side of his command deck to study the space before him. Through the viewport, the *R'nalz* and *Tezner* proceeded beside them.

Curious, he studied the holographic display of every sensor. He read the report, stunned to see the Zaguarz planetary defense system destroyed along with many of their crops. The Zaguarz were tribal, less technical, dealing with agriculture and exportation through the arkross and various merchant vessels. Ships were not something they could build on their own, so they relied on their planet defense system.

Pirates were awful, but they were above this brutality. Not to mention, they lacked the capacity and power to get away with something on this scale. Especially against the Zaguarz. This wasn't theft. It was domination. No wonder they hadn't heard from the tribal species.

Kaytrix focused on the planet before him, the eerie feeling growing. He studied the mutilated planet, hoping for another clue. That's when a silhouette emerged in the planet's shadow. Was it debris or a ship?

"Scan the planet and surrounding space for any energy signatures," he ordered.

"There's nothing there, Commander," reported Kersa after a moment.

He fidgeted with his cape's clasp. Could he be mistaken? His instincts warned him not to believe the readings. He needed to be sure.

"Take us closer to investigate and have weapons on standby. Continue to scan."

"Yes, sir. Adjusting heading now," his pilot, Auss, responded.

"Inform the other ship's commanders of our intentions and have them follow at a distance," he ordered. If the enemy was here, he didn't want to endanger the other ships.

Communication's Officer Satki followed his command, and he could hear her muttering his words over the comm.

The *Ro'arck* proceeded forward. He observed the space before them, scrutinizing the shadows for the silhouette.

"Commander, I am detecting faint energy readings," Kersa said.

"What kind?" He glanced to Kersa as she scanned over the information on her terminal's screen.

"Unknown, Commander. Nothing compares to it in our database," she said, her tone fearful.

Her answer proved his suspicions true. There *was* something there. The only thing left to discover is if it was the same ship from O'ber.

As they neared the object the bridge fell silent. The entire ship was black, with eight sharp points jutting out of its top and curling back underneath. Round pearly spheres stared back at them—viewports to the command bridge, no doubt.

"Hold position here," he commanded.

Uncertainty crept into his soul. He had never dealt with a situation like this before. Should he try to contact them? After a moment of hesitation, a row of green lights grew in brilliance along the hull. Their sudden appearance revealed the true size of the ship. It was a monster compared to the *Ro'arck*.

"Commander, an increase of energy has spiked across the ship's forward section," Kersa said. She gazed at her screen, absorbing the data before her.

He didn't want to assume this energy reading was weapons, but what else could it be?

"Should we prepare to fire?" asked Zenro.

"Increase shield strength to our forward sections. I don't want to fire first in case we get this wrong," he said.

"Energy levels are continuing to increase, Commander," Kersa said.

Her stressed voice worried him, but before he could utter a command, a wave of cannon fire emitted from the dark ship. The fire struck their shields and damaged some out of the outer hull. He struggled to breathe. Even with their new vessels, the enemy's weapons were stronger.

"Evasive action and return fire! Tell the *R'nalz* and *Tezner* to abort, Satki!" He recognized the green blasts of energy. This was the same ship that had laid waste to the camp at O'ber. After witnessing their power firsthand, he wasn't taking any chances with the *Tezner* and *R'nalz*.

"Commander, both ships have weakened shields and are sustaining heavy damage!" reported Kersa.

"That's impossible!" He covered his mouth, struggling to believe what he was hearing. Their specs on his holo-screen indicated her report was true, but how? "Tell them to abort now. Why haven't we lost shields?" he asked.

"They received direct hits while it only grazed us, sir," Levro said.

Another wave of green energy hit them and the sister ships.

"Sir, I have readings indicating they are launching escape pods," Levro said. "They've lost engines and other systems are failing."

Kaytrix ground his teeth. How were they failing so quickly? Being a starship commander wasn't what he thought it would be.

"We are coming around the vessel's side, Commander. Your orders?" asked Auss, his voice thick with urgency. Kaytrix noted how he handled the *Ro'arck*. Auss kept looking back at him instead of focusing on where he was going, showing his inexperience.

His stomach knotted and an inescapable heat rose throughout his body. He'd hoped Auss would have some instinct on what to do. "Come about! On our way to the sister ships, we will attack the enemy. Have our rescue shuttles on standby to retrieve the pods. Fire when ready!"

Blasts of blue energy ripped from the *Ro'arck's* gun ports. The projectiles collided with the black ship. Green shields rippled across the surface in response, mocking their attempts.

Kaytrix clenched his jaw as a memory of firing at the soldier on O'ber surfaced. There was no mistaking them now. These were the same perpetrators responsible for taking so many Archarian lives.

"They appear heavily shielded," reported Zenro. He paused at his station and his eyes ran over his screens with a look of confusion.

Kaytrix ground his teeth. "Zenro, you must keep firing."

"The enemy is launching fighters and attacking the escape pods!" Levro said.

"Target their fighters and keep trying to weaken their shields."

"Commander, we are approaching the *R'nalz* and *Tezner*," reported Auss.

Kaytrix inhaled. He needed to get used to the flood of reports. "Launch the shuttles at once with support of our fighters!" he commanded.

The sight before him was dreadful. Pieces of debris from their ships floated in space, suspended horrifically in a state of limbo.

"Commander, two Varanus ships are approaching," Kersa said.

Kaytrix's holo-screen displayed the large ships moving in. "We didn't call for them to aid us, but we could use the assistance. Keep course," he ordered. "Satki, ask the Varanus vessels to attack the enemy while we recover the pods."

"Sir, the Varanus are opening fire on the *R'nalz* and *Tezner*!" Kersa shrieked.

"What?!" Through the viewport, the massive Varanus ships fired on the vulnerable Archarian ships. The attack was swift and aggressive.

Kaytrix tightened his fists. How dare they!

The *Ro'arck* shook from a weapon strike. Systems wailed in warning.

"Commander, our shields are sustaining damage. We will not survive more strikes!" Tuce, his technology specialist, announced. His screen shone a bright yellow on his face, solidifying his statement. Systems were on the brink of failure.

"Try to reroute some unnecessary power to the shields to buy us time," Kaytrix suggested.

"What systems should I bypass?" Tuce asked.

A touch of annoyance knitted Kaytrix's brow. Didn't Tuce know how to make executive decisions? "Try rerouting power from the jump drive," he suggested.

A wave of helplessness overcame him. Not only was he dealing with an inexperienced crew, but their best technology was failing, and their allies had turned against them.

"Your orders?" Levro shouted, desperation in his voice.

"Continue course for the *R'nalz* and *Tezner* wreckage. We must save as many Archarians as we can."

"And the Varanus?" Levro asked.

"They made their choice. All batteries, open fire!" Kaytrix growled. Many Varanus leaders had joined them at their table in the past. Fighting against each other now was a punch to the gut he hadn't anticipated.

The *Ro'arck* flew through space, and Auss positioned her between the Varanus and the sister ships. The shuttles started their retrieval of the pods beneath the shelter of the *Ro'arck* while the Archarian fighters fought to keep the enemy from destroying the vulnerable pods.

Kaytrix observed the pilots' skills as they flew in packs. The Archarian fighters were swift, swirling around the shuttles and protecting them from the attacking enemy. The dogfight intensified as more enemy fighters joined the battle. Their proximity to the *Ro'arck* was increasing when an enemy fighter disintegrated in front of the main viewport. Kaytrix stepped back, startled by the sudden explosion.

"The enemy's fighters lack shielding," Levro announced, his tone optimistic.

"Locate their hangar and wreak havoc on it. Prevent them from launching more fighters," Kaytrix growled. If he couldn't attack the ship directly, he'd settle for destroying their fighters.

"Sir, we have recovered most of the pods. The shuttles are on their way back and our fighters continue to engage the enemy," Levro reported.

Kaytrix reassessed the confrontation. The black ship remained distant, as if letting the Varanus vessels take the brunt of losses. He prowled to the opposite end of the command bridge.

"Continue with our attack, Zenro. Protect our shuttles at all costs." He clenched his teeth. They might survive this, but he had not forgotten their shield's status. They had sustained two hits from the enemy's main cannon and they were on the verge of losing their shields, but he couldn't leave the shuttles and pods behind.

"Sir, the shuttles have docked safely and most of our fighters are intact," Levro said.

"Have the fighters return to the hangar, and set a course for home. We must retreat," he ordered with bitterness. He hated to leave this mission with no answers as to what happened to the Zaguarz or who this enemy was, but there was no victory in getting slaughtered.

"Yes, sir. Engaging hyperspace jump when ready, sir," Auss said.

"The fighters have returned to the hangar," Levro stated.

The black vessel charged its main cannon, anticipating their escape.

"Engage the jump!" Kaytrix grasped the arms of his command chair in anticipation.

A portal opened directly in front of them and the *Ro'arck* proceeded through, narrowly avoiding the enemy's last attack, which could have ended their lives.

Kaytrix let out a sigh, feeling defeated. How could the enemy inflict so much damage on their best starships? Why had the Varanus turned against them after millennia of being part of the alliance? And the Zaguarz . . . Were they to be lost forever?

The *Ro'arck* limped to the space station while he sorted through the events. The admiral was not going to be pleased with these results.

"Approaching the *Narvent*," Levro announced. "Shall I dock to have repairs started?"

Kaytrix nodded while skimming a report of the ship's systems. Many systems blazed yellow and red while only a handful held the green status of *undamaged*.

"Satki, hail Admiral Ackon on the holo-screen. I need to speak to him."

"Yes, sir," Satki said, making the connection.

In moments, the face of the admiral appeared in a blue luminous light. "Status report?" he asked.

"The Zaguarz are under siege from the same enemy as O'ber," Kaytrix said. "We encountered one hostile ship and are unaware of the other's location, sir. I regret to report we lost both the *Tezner* and *R'nalz*."

Ackon looked displeased. "That is unfortunate news, Commander."

Kaytrix's jaw tightened. "There's more, sir. Several Varanus ships attacked us and participated in the destruction of the sister ships. The extent of their allegiance change is unknown."

The admiral's face grew pale and there was a moment of silence. "It is important this news does not reach the surface of Archaria, understand?"

"Yes, sir." Kaytrix acknowledged the order, but it was confusing. They were always honest with the public. Why were they keeping information from them now?

"If the people find out, it will cause mass hysteria," Admiral Ackon continued. "Return to Avsilan at once. We need to discuss our next course of action with the council."

The hologram deactivated.

The admiral's request made sense. Archaria lead the alliance as the chief protector of the galaxy. If their allies discovered they could not defend themselves, it would endanger their allegiance. Their allies relied on them for protection; without that, Archaria lost her seniority as protector and peacekeeper. Archaria could not afford to fail her allies. Not if this skirmish turned into a war. But lying to them wasn't the right course of action either.

Kaytrix let the details of the confrontation drift away and observed his crew. They appeared worn from the chaotic battle and gazed at him solemnly, awaiting orders.

"Attention, everyone," he said. "It is imperative the events of today remain unspoken until I have a chance to speak to the council. Understood?"

The crew nodded and busied themselves with their tasks.

The *Ro'arck* finished docking, creating a seal between it and the *Narvent*. Kaytrix gathered the sensors' data and directed a copy to command. They could further analyze the data and hopefully learn something useful about their enemy.

"Lieutenant Levro," he called, motioning with his hand.

"Yes, sir?" Levro stood waiting.

"I must leave to the surface. I trust you to oversee the repairs and to tend to any issues that might arise while I am gone. Here's the data crystal the *Narvent* repair crew will need. See to it they get it."

"Y-yes, sir." Levro smiled, a hint of a sparkle in his eye.

Kaytrix patted his arm. "If you need something, hail me?"

"Yes, sir."

He hated to leave his crew in this state—terrified, worried, and in shock—but the admiral required his presence. What happened today had never happened in the history of the Archarians. The death toll alone was astounding.

Kaytrix wished he could aid the transport of the *Tezner* and *R'nalz* survivors to the *Narvent's* medical center. It would be hard to face them, knowing that how the mission ended was his fault. He hoped to never lose that many lives again, but deep down, a realization tugged on him. It was possible to fail again, and it meant more blood on his hands.

He took the *Narvent* lift to the arkross. This moment of urgency to return to Avsilan was a welcome distraction from the brutal mission.

Questions for the council bubbled in his mind. Would they call the alliance together and address the Varanus attacking their ships? The alliance did not take treachery lightly. Would they make the allies aware of their vulnerability to this enemy?

He hoped the councillors were in a better mood than he was. In the back of his skull, a searing irritation grew. He wasn't used to this kind of failure.

The portal's activation sequence began with swirling energy rising from the arkross to prepare for his travel. In a few moments, it settled, awaiting his passage.

Kaytrix walked through the glowing energy and appeared on the other side in Avsilan. He acknowledged the guards and proceeded to the council chambers with haste. What he was about to tell his leaders would scar their history for eons to come.

Chapter 5

SECRETS AND SCHEMES

Kaytrix analyzed the events of the battle, preparing to face his leaders with the facts. But how could he tell his superiors that the pride of their fleet was no match for one ship?

The lift opened with a sudden rush, startling him. He tried to remember everything of importance as he passed through the wooden doors to the council chamber. Harsh words echoed in the heights of the room. He paused his approach and peered around the doorway.

"I warned you about this," Admiral Ackon said with bitterness. He was looking at Perseph. "We wouldn't be in this predicament if we told the allies the truth."

"I concur, Admiral," Karva replied. "Our society stands of the brink of collapse, and our allies are not aware of the threat." He took in a breath as though to calm himself. "We should never have let it go this far. We must ask the allies to join in the fight."

"It's not that difficult to follow the plan, Karva." Perseph groaned. "Keep your damn cool and the plan will work out. You will see."

"Draining our resources to prevent a war was never a part of our plan!" Karva fumed. "We made mistakes. Why keep burying them with new schemes?"

"We don't need the allies to know of our failed endeavors," Sarneft spat. "We needed someone to take the responsibility. That's why we chose Commander Torex. Follow the plan!"

"You and your damn pride," Karva snapped. "If we wait any longer, it will be too late!"

"After mission 3199 and 3200, are you really in the position to make recommendations, *Farmer*?" Perseph asked.

There was silence.

Kaytrix turned away, his heart tightening in his chest. Of what war did they speak? Wasn't the confrontation just starting? Why was he chosen? How he wanted to wake from this nightmare, but his armor's weight and the stench of his sweat brought him back to reality.

He cleared his throat and rounded the corner, coming into view of the councillors and the admiral facing each other in a tight circle.

"Commander, you are early," Perseph stated in annoyance.

Kaytrix continued his approach, sharing a look with the admiral. "The admiral made it clear this was an urgent matter."

Perseph scowled and sat down. "Indeed, it is."

The others sat down as Kaytrix took his place in the middle of the crescent table.

"Let's begin." Sarneft nodded, her face irritated.

Kaytrix exhaled. It was difficult to focus on what he needed to say. Their private conversation angered him. How could they pretend everything was fine when it clearly wasn't? And if Archaria was running low on resources, it meant an economic collapse. He still didn't know how this was possible.

The council watched him with expectant faces. As the moments passed, worry ate away at their eyes. Their silent tension escalated until he spoke.

"The enemy destroyed two of our fleet's most advanced ships with the aid of Varanus vessels," Kaytrix said. "I am here to announce that a race within our controlled space rivals our technology—dare I say, surpasses it."

"Do you have evidence?" Perseph asked.

The question caught Kaytrix off guard. "Do you think I speak of this lightly? How can you demand evidence when you can clearly see the loss in our command center?" He took in a slow breath, but it did nothing against the anger churning inside of him.

"My apologies for being unclear, Commander," Perseph said. He looked amused at Kaytrix's lack of control. "I meant evidence for the treachery of the Varanus."

Perseph's apology was empty.

"I can only report that two vessels attacked. Whether the rest of Varanus follow their lead needs to be investigated," Kaytrix said, crossing his arms. Was Perseph purposefully toying with him? He remembered what they said about choosing him. Was it because of his reputation of having a bad temper?

"It is obvious we can't trust the Varanus," Admiral Ackon said. "Data from the *Ro'arck* proves that. Our next move is to recover their arkross to prevent further invasions to other planets. I think we can assume we've lost the Zaguarz to the enemy."

The admiral's decision unhinged his jaw and stirred his anger. The acts of a few Varanus did not define the stance of the rest, and giving up on Zaguarz so soon? "I disagree, Admiral. How are we sure the Varanus have turned against us? These could have been rogue ships, even stolen."

Ackon's face soured into a frown. "We can't take the time to investigate this. The enemy is spreading and if the Varanus are on their side, we must not delay. You will command the *Ro'arck* to Varanus and retrieve their arkross. I will have ships on standby to assist you if you need reinforcements."

Kaytrix fidgeted with the edge of his cloak. He was uncomfortable with this tactic. "If we turn our backs on them without a solid reason, we could be making the mistake of a lifetime."

Admiral Ackon slammed his fist on the table. "Don't question orders, Kaytrix! If they have turned, their might mixed with the enemy's will doom us all. We can't take that chance. We must act swiftly and hope that they forgive us later for our sudden decisions."

Kaytrix stood tall. He didn't regret questioning the decision. He didn't want to go through with this mission, but if he had to, he needed experienced crew members on the *Ro'arck*. Another battle like the last, and they were as good as drorse fodder.

"Understood, Admiral. Sir, if this is your chosen course of action, may I recommend seasoned personnel stationed on the *Ro'arck*? It will increase our chances of success. My weapons officer, pilot, and technology specialist are capable but inexperienced for this level of intensity."

Admiral Ackon sighed and in a calm voice said, "That is acceptable. We can't risk more mistakes, but we also cannot delay. I will see what I can do. Now, return to the *Ro'arck* and prepare for this mission, with or without your requested crew." Ackon folded his hands.

"Understood, sir." Kaytrix said, glad the admiral would consider his request. "Sir, may I add that if we had called the allies for support, we would have had an advantage. Acting alone is costing us."

Ackon crossed his arms, shooting him a look. "Duly noted, Commander. But there's no need to unsettle them with something we can handle alone."

Kaytrix could sense the admiral's irritation. "I will see to my orders," he said and turned to leave.

The council chamber doors closed behind Kaytrix, and his anger rose to the surface. He stormed across the marbled floors to the lift and slammed the destination panel with a fist. Why did the council see fit to abandon the Varanus? What was happening to the resources of Archaria? And their conversation . . . what responsibility did they want him to have?

Being a commander of a starship had always been his dream, but he couldn't help feeling he was a pawn in the council's eyes. He needed to find out what was going on to protect the alliance, Archaria, and his parents, but who could he trust with his feelings?

If he wanted to find answers, the only place he could find them was in the archives. Anyone could access the knowledge in the public database from missions, officer promotions, expenses, and supply allocation.

His finger hovered over the cracked panel as he hesitated. The admiral had ordered him to return to the *Ro'arck* and prepare for his mission, yet something in his heart told him he needed to know what the council was talking about. To find the truth, he needed to disobey his orders.

Kaytrix bit his lip as he contemplated his choice. He couldn't think of just himself and his family anymore. He needed to think of Archaria and the alliance what was best for them. He selected the archives, hoping his suspicions about the council were wrong. He desperately wanted to believe that he misheard them, that it was all a dream.

Riding in the lift was a slight distraction as he observed the city through the glass. In the distance, snowy mountains stood against the horizon, catching the rays of dawn. It was a magnificent sight. He exhaled, calmed by the scenery.

The longer he gazed out the window, the more he missed the comforts of home and the ridiculous dessert his ma made.

The lift traveled to the lower levels and a fog enveloped the city buildings. He scoffed, his mood darkening as the lift penetrated the fog and plunged into the darker depths. He found the scene symbolic. On the surface, Archaria basked in the light of success, but beneath she was falling into despair.

When the lift opened, he took a confident step out. He'd been on this level many times while attending the Warrior Academy. This level appeared the same as the others except for the open entranceway leading into the archive.

Through the arched opening stood isles and isles of shimmering blue data crystals stacked upon each other in towers of light. These towers were as high as the ceiling. Their length extended through the entire space, making the archives feel more like a maze of light. Each row started at the center of the room, where a round orb floated. In front of this orb were sections for people to sit and listen to information. Alternatively, they could manually search the archive for the information they sought.

He passed through the entrance, remembering that an archive keeper usually lingered around. He needed to avoid them at all costs. What he was looking into didn't need to be common knowledge.

He approached a section of the archive, passing the glowing blue orb of random holographic knowledge. There was not a soul to be seen in the archives at this hour, and for that he was grateful. He quickened his pace as he glided to a section of crystals. He studied them for a second when he accessed the search interface. A holo-screen appeared, and he keyed in his search.

First, he searched the archives for recent missions to O'ber. He added the names of officers he met stationed there such as Captain Wesk and Commander Dest. Well over a thousand documents appeared, the majority dated from before he was in the Warrior Academy. How could that be?

A slight surge of success radiated through him. He tapped the screen and selected a document, eager to devour the information. But upon opening the file, a message displayed across his screen in bold red: "access code required."

He selected another file. This one had sections edited out. Everything the council approved for the planet O'ber they kept hidden from the public. Decoding the files would take time and skill he didn't have, but he needed to know what the council was hiding. In the moment, he could transfer the data and hope he could access the contents later. He touched the screen, copying the files to his gauntlet.

Sweat beaded on his forehead as the progress bar crept across his screen. He hadn't anticipated it would take this long. Once the transfer completed, he moved with haste to disconnect from the terminal.

As he stood to leave, his eyes caught files numbered 3199 and 3200 under his O'ber search. They were the files Perseph mentioned. Filled with curiosity, he selected the first file. He grew nervous as the crystal panel entered the reader. The time to deviate from boarding the *Ro'arck* dwindled, yet he found himself pulled toward these files.

The information projected onto the holo-screen in an instant. To his surprise, this report did not need an access code. He read the standard details of the report: ship name, commander . . . But the mission description section of the report was blank.

Kaytrix scoffed. Of course, it was. He flicked to the end of the file, his heart pounding as his time in the archive ticked away. He scrolled through the editorial history tabs. There were two entries recorded—one was the creation of the file, and the second was an edit. His heart stopped as he read when the missions happened. The date must have been incorrect. He exited 3199 and selected 3200. It was the same, dated 110 solar rotations ago. That was before he was born!

A sudden clash in the archive broke his concentration. He jumped and in a frenzied moment, unloaded the crystal panel and cleared his search history. He feared the noise was the archive keeper. The last thing he needed was an inquisitive Archarian trying to help him out.

Kaytrix slipped to the side of the archive tower and peered around the corner. The orb in the center continued to spin and there was no one in the hallway outside. He turned to look down the aisle beside him. The archive keepers' white robes crumpled as they stooped to retrieve a broken vase from the floor.

Kaytrix snuck toward the exit, taking care to place his feet softly. He made it to the exit and proceeded to the lift without being noticed. The lift door closed, and he sighed with relief. He still didn't have any clear answers, but now he knew the council was hiding something. He needed to find out what it was and how he played into their schemes.

Chapter 6

RECRUITS

Sitting in the command center of the *Ro'arck*, Kaytrix struggled to focus on his tasks. Current events weighed heavily on his mind. What was he going to do about the council? Letting their decisions continue to threaten the integrity of Archaria wasn't an option, but he wasn't sure what could be done.

He took a moment to gaze at his beautiful home planet. He couldn't bear to stand on the sidelines and watch it crumble, but could he risk everything he'd ever worked for to protect it?

He studied his engagement with the enemy. There was something to be learnt from the recordings like a weakness in the ship.

Half of a rotation passed as he analyzed the data, and he remembered the blade from O'ber. Did the scientists find anything useful in the analysis? He would be sure to ask the admiral next time.

He looked up from his work to muse, his gaze falling on Lieutenant Levro, noting his furrowed brow and the crew's anxious faces as they worked. They took his constructive criticism hard but appeared to fully understand his reasonings. In fact, they appeared determined to do better this time around, especially if experienced crew joined them.

In his peripheral vision, several Archarian starships appeared from a hyperspace jump. These must be the reinforcements Admiral Ackon had mentioned. He counted the older vessels. There were three. Only three. He hoped he wouldn't need to call upon them for help at Varanus.

"Sir," Satki interrupted. "I am receiving a message from the admiral. He says, 'Your requested recruits are on their way to the *Narvent*. See to it they get familiar with their stations while repairs are underway.'"

Kaytrix nodded. "Thank you, Satki. I will go meet them now. Lieutenant Levro." He turned to face the younger man pouring over various reports. "You are in charge until I return."

Levro saluted. "Yes, sir."

Kaytrix took the lift to the *Narvent*. He hoped these new recruits, whoever they were, could bring the experience he needed on the bridge. He also worried how they'd feel taking orders from him. As much as his title had changed, who he was as a person had not. He was still from the Farmer clan, even though he'd rightfully earned his place among the Warrior clan.

Kaytrix entered the lift and proceeded through the pressurized room. Once the light turned green, he entered the access corridor to the *Narvent*. The gray tunnel and white lights welcomed his arrival while the coldness of space found the nape of his neck. He pulled his cloak up closer for warmth.

He approached the last set of doors when they whizzed apart, revealing Karrin standing with three faces he recognized. They had aged, but there was no mistaking them.

"Mac! Nat! Drozah! What are you doing here?"

Drozah pressed past Karrin and embraced him in a hug. "You're the one who asked for experienced personnel. What? You didn't think they would send the best?"

Kaytrix tried to laugh, but Drozah's hold on him was too tight.

"Stop it, Drozah. His eyeballs are about to pop out of his head!" Mac forced his hands between Drozah's large brown arms and Kaytrix's body only to embrace him as well.

"So good to see you, Kaytrix!" He stepped back to look at him. "So, you are commanding your own ship now? When did that happen?" Mac looked him up and down with a wry smile. "Did you buy your way in?"

Kaytrix's cheeks flushed. "No," he retorted.

Mac laughed, slapping his knee. He was a crude, thin man from the Creative clan who tamed his wiry red hair into a braid along the crest of his head. His skillset in technology and his ability to adapt to demanding circumstances made him an exceptional soldier.

"I'll have you know the council promoted me," Kaytrix added.

"So that makes it legit, right?" Drozah laughed, high-fiving Mac.

Kaytrix laughed as well, having missed the banter of his friends. They had grown up in the same village, and in a small way they had become a part of each other's families.

He locked eyes with Nat as she stood on the side, as if letting the rowdy guys get their testosterone out. She was one of the few starship fliers able to pilot a vessel without the aid and calculations of their AI systems. It made her versatile and sought after by every commander.

He smiled and she smiled back. The flutter of butterflies in his stomach was instant. How he missed her. "Nat," he said fondly, embracing her. "How have you been?"

She tucked a delicate curl of burgundy hair behind her ear. "Well, life's been interesting, but I am glad to have a change. What's going on here?" Her soft brown eyes shone bright under the lights of the corridor.

Kaytrix indicated the *Ro'arck* behind him. "I'm commanding this beauty, but my crew needs some guidance. The situation we got into was more intense than their training prepared them for. That's why I requested some additional help. Did the admiral debrief you before you arrived?" It occurred to Kaytrix what it meant to see his friends here. As glad as he was to see them after ten solar rotations, this was not the reunion he had envisioned. His mission was dangerous.

"He did in a very rushed sort of way," Mac said, stroking his scraggly beard. "I have a feeling he left some key details out."

"Very well. I will fill you in. As you can see, the *Ro'arck*'s repairs are underway from our last encounter with the enemy." He pointed to the *Ro'arck* as little repair drones worked to fix hull damage. "We lost the

R'nalz and *Tezner* in a matter of moments. The ship we faced is a force to be reckoned with. Their ability to challenge our technology makes them a threat. One to respect," he continued.

"Sounds like we finally have a challenge for a change," Drozah said, a spark of zeal in his eyes.

Kaytrix found himself angry at his large, bearded friend. "We've lost lives, Drozah. Thousands of lives. This isn't an opportunity to flex your might. Am I clear?"

Drozah snapped a salute. "Yes, sir!"

Of course, it was his friend's nature to love weapons and heavy artillery, to hunger for a fight. It was his specialty. But Drozah would have to learn the same life lesson he had. Losing the *Tezner* and *R'nalz* was not the adventure they dreamed of as children. Adventure was one thing. This was slaughter.

He turned toward the *Ro'arck* and headed back to the ship. "I will introduce you to your stations. Familiarize yourselves with them. We have a limited amount of time before we begin our next mission."

"Yes, sir," they answered.

"What is our next mission?" asked Nat.

He stopped to study their faces before exiting the corridor. They waited for an answer. He needed them aboard the *Ro'arck*, but part of him wished he could turn them away. Once they crossed the airlock threshold, there was no going back.

"Two Varanus ships attacked us. As a result, we are taking back their arkross," he said.

Mac's jaw dropped. "That's never happened before! Every planet our ancestors gifted an arkross to still has it. Is the admiral certain this is what he wants to do?"

Kaytrix crossed his arms. "The admiral and the council are determined this is the only way."

"That'll piss off the Varanus," Drozah huffed.

Kaytrix paced down the corridor and back toward them, still feeling conflicted about their involvement.

"What is it?" Nat asked. She was always so perceptive.

"I'll be honest with you. Things around here lately are not what they seem."

He told them everything from O'ber to what he found in the archives. Their internal struggle was obvious as their forms turned rigid. No one wanted to hear that what they fought for and believed in was at a risk.

"What are we going to do?" Mac asked.

"I don't know yet. Come on, I will show you your stations."

He led the group through the pressurized chamber, through the corridors, and onto the bridge deck. Several of the bridge crew greeted them with salutes from their stations.

Lieutenant Levro approached and saluted. "Commander, repairs are nearing completion."

"Well done. Anything else to report?" Kaytrix asked.

"Nothing, sir, but the repair crews have been asking questions," Levro stated in a hushed tone.

Kaytrix scowled as he remembered the conversation he overheard from the councillors. It was a bitter reminder that he was partaking in their deceit.

"I am hoping we can share the truth with them soon," he said. He laid a hand on Levro's shoulder and tried to be reassuring.

"Yes, sir."

He turned toward his friends. "Lieutenant, these are the new officers to be stationed on the *Ro'arck*. Technology Specialist Mac Secu, Pilot Nat Rivkah, and Weapons Expert Drozah Dura. They will fight alongside us from now on."

"It's a pleasure to meet you." Levro saluted. "Sir," he said, turning to face him. "May I show them their stations?"

He nodded. Levro lead his friends onto the deck, introducing them to the rest of the crew. Allowing his friends to join him on this mission was the right decision. Their presence was hope for his crew—a hope they desperately needed.

Chapter 7

PLANET VARANUS

Kaytrix awoke from his meditative sleep to the buzz of his comm in his inner ear.

"Commander Torex," he answered, running a hand over his exhausted face. He listened intently and rose from the chair he had collapsed on in his private quarters. "Thank you, Zilas," he said.

He deactivated the link and rushed to his sink to splash water onto his face. The *Narvent* crew had completed their repairs on the *Ro'arck*, and it was time to embark on their mission.

Kaytrix dressed in his armor, attaching his cloak as the last piece before heading to the bridge. When he entered, Nat sat in the pilot's chair. The other stations were empty.

"Something wrong?" she asked as she turned to look at him.

"It's time, Nat," he said as he activated the ship's internal communications. "Crew of the *Ro'arck*, report to your stations."

He settled into the command chair and readied systems. From his seat, he could remotely access every system on the bridge via a holo-screen.

The stillness faded, replaced by the bustling of crew members as they rushed to their stations. Each of them settled into their places, appearing nervous.

Kaytrix tried to exude confidence, though he shared in their apprehension. This wasn't going to be a simple mission. He had studied the Varanus extensively while at the academy and had witnessed their fortitude multiple times. They were a mighty and fierce race brought up in various clans that lived for the hunt. Not only was their appearance menacing with their height and muscular bodies, but their cunning intelligence matched their ferocity. What they lacked in advancements, they made up for in numbers. He hoped the *Ro'arck* would not have to fight them.

"Systems are ready," Levro announced at his holo-screen. A soft green light highlighted his cheekbones.

"Thank you, Lieutenant."

Kaytrix overlooked the space before them. It was like looking at a blank canvas. Endless possibilities and outcomes awaited him, all hinging on his decisions. For the first time, he questioned everything he stood for. Was he fighting for Archaria? For the alliance? Or for those in power?

His nerves escalated. He couldn't be more prepared than he was, and yet uncertainty crept in from the years of shaming and belittling. He thought of the commander he had punched, whose words had carved a permanent scar into his mind, echoing like shattering glass: "You will always be inferior, no matter what you accomplish."

In his heart, he knew that statement was wrong. Sitting here among the stars was evidence enough. He worked harder than anyone else, determined to surge ahead. Sure, he was uncertain of this mission's outcome, not only for what would happen between them and the Varanus, but what these actions would mean for the rest of the alliance. But just like in any other confrontation he had faced, he would do his best to overcome his uncertainty.

"Let's disembark," he said.

Lieutenant Levro set to work effortlessly at his console to begin the process. "The *Narvent* has successfully detached," he said.

"I have set a course for Varanus. Standing by to engage the jump upon optimal distance," Nat announced from her pilot's seat beside Auss.

A moment passed while Kaytrix overlooked their progress on his display. The *Ro'arck* reached its distance from the *Narvent* to travel. They were ready.

"Engage the jump when ready, Nat."

Nat nodded and pushed in a sequence of commands.

The fiery blue portal open before them. The *Ro'arck* proceeded through and arrived at the coordinates. In the distance waited Varanus, a planet of green vegetation, abundant with oceans, seas, and lakes. In her orbit, several large Varanus ships prowled.

"Shield is holding at optimal levels, Commander," Mac announced. "What are your orders?"

Kaytrix expected to see Varanus ships surrounding the planet, but it didn't hurt to check for their new enemy either.

"Ensure our new enemy isn't somewhere nearby. I don't want to repeat our last encounter," he growled, his failure still fresh.

Kaytrix stared into the space before him and checked his screens, but unlike before, there was no black shadow. He stood to pace the bridge, his eyes locked on the viewport and the planet framed within it. "Keep our approach at a steady speed," he said, pacing. "As soon as we get close enough, search for the location of the arkross."

As they neared the spinning planet, the air thickened with anticipation.

"Sir!" Kersa cried out. "I have detected several Varanus ships fighting in orbit."

"Against the new enemy?" he asked.

"Against each other, Commander." She stared at her screen in horror. "It's a massive battle on the far side of the planet. That's why we couldn't detect it at first."

A surge of hope rose in him. If there was a chance Varanus still stood with them in the alliance, he had to take it. He needed to investigate what was happening before following through with his orders.

"Get us closer to the planet. Engage shields and try to contact Varanus. See if we can lend them a hand."

"But Commander, what about our mission?" Levro asked, his brow furrowed. The idea of disobeying orders obviously did not sit well with him.

The rest of the crew watched on.

"Lieutenant, there's no reason to take the arkross if Varanus still stands with us. We need to know what is happening before we proceed."

There was a moment of silence. Levro studied his face as if searching for the reasoning behind the decision.

"Yes, sir." Levro nodded.

Kaytrix let out a breath he'd been holding. The crew viewed Levro as a compass, their loyalty to Archaria strong. He would have to be careful in sharing his views of the council around them.

"Sir," said Satki. "His Excellence, Hakte, is ready to speak to you."

Kaytrix sat in his command chair and his nervousness returned. He'd never spoken to the Varanus representative before. "Thank you, Satki. Put it up."

In a sudden flash of Kaytrix's holographic display, Hakte's face appeared before him. "Archarian Commander, we are grateful to see your ship in our space." His blue tongue slithered between his fine teeth. "Your presence comes at a time of our greatest need."

Kaytrix noted the worry in the knotted brow of the Varanus. "What's happening, Your Excellence?"

"War has erupted between the clans. The strongest of us fight our brethren, but something wicked has possessed their spirits. We are collapsing beneath their unknown source of power."

Kaytrix pressed a hand to his chest, the news devastating. "How can I be of assistance, Your Excellence?"

"Our forces have fended off their attack for now, but it won't be long before they seize more ships. Their leader is aboard one ship in orbit. We have determined which clans have bought into his lies of a superior race in the galaxy, one that will lead us to a position of greatness. He has pledged to follow this race called the Nevo."

Kaytrix tightened his fists at the name of his new enemy. So that's what the Varanus were promised in return for their betrayal to the alliance: greatness. He ground his teeth, picturing the soldier at O'ber, the soldier called a Nevo.

"Your Excellence, we will do everything in our power to protect you."

"Thank you, Commander. I—"

The connection turned fuzzy and Hakte's face disappeared. Kaytrix could only assume the enemy had taken out their communications. They needed to hurry if they were to make a difference.

He drew in a breath. "Inform the admiral of our intentions, Satki. Take us in and open fire on the Varanus rebels. Lieutenant, launch fighter squads 1 to 3 and have them aid our allies."

They rounded the massive planet, coming upon the full extent of the battle. Wreckage of lost ships floated in the planet's orbit. It was a living graveyard. The Varanus had destroyed many ships in attempts to stop the takeover. Kaytrix cringed as a Varanus body floated by the viewport.

The holo-screen to his left displayed squads of fighters rushing out of their hangar bay and into the fight. Their sudden appearance aggravated the Varanus vessels, and their ships gravitated toward the *Ro'arck*.

"Sir, the admiral has sent us reinforcements. Three sister ships join in our attack," Satki announced.

"Alright, get them to form up beside us. We will take on the rebel Varanus ships together."

In his holo-screen, the three sister ships joined their vessel. He was confident they could save Varanus from this rebel faction, but what did Hakte mean when he said they had an unknown source of power?

"We are being targeted," Kersa announced.

As they surged toward the battlefield, several blasts hit their shields. The Varanus were formidable opponents, but for the *Ro'arck's* class of ship, their attacks were merely jabs.

Kaytrix observed the battlefield, noting that one Varanus ship appeared to linger behind. No doubt the leader of the rebel Varanus was on that ship.

"Target the closest enemy. Fire!"

Blue energy ripped from the Archarian ships and pelted the ships of the Varanus. Ripples of energy danced across their surfaces as the energy penetrated and struck their targets. The closest ship fell toward the planet as its engines failed and burned upon re-entry. Kaytrix focused on the remaining ships.

"Target the next ship and continue firing. We need to end this here."

"Commander," Levro said. He stared uneasily at his screen, his face filled with fear.

It caught Kaytrix off guard. What could be wrong? A chill ran up his spine as a black ship approached from behind the rebel Varanus ships, laying waste to any opposition from the planet and their allied Varanus.

Kaytrix tensed. His anger heightened as flashes of his squad falling at O'ber and the destruction of the *Tezner* and *R'nalz* resurfaced.

It was the Nevo ship.

"Forget the rebel Varanus. Target the Nevo ship with everything we have."

The sister ships attacked with a force strong enough to destroy several Varanus ships three times over, but the enemy vessel stood fast, its shields still intact.

Panic surged in Kaytrix as the Nevo ship open fire. "Tell the sister ships to abort now!" he roared. "Refocus our attack on the primary weapon, everything we have!"

The strain of battle returned as the Archarian ships turned to leave. The older class of vessels moved slower and took fire from the Nevo ship. Kaytrix clenched his jaw.

"Move us to intercept the attack. Try to protect their retreat," he ordered, but Nat had already begun the process, seeming to anticipate his order before he gave it.

Three blasts hit the *Ro'arck*, but it wasn't enough. Kaytrix could see one ship ripping apart as escape pods jettisoned into the surrounding space. The other ships successfully entered jump space unscathed.

"Sir, enemy fighters are entering the debris field. They are destroying the escape pods!" Levro exclaimed.

Kaytrix was getting a proper sense of how this enemy worked. They learnt from their last encounter that he valued life over victory. They were testing him now to see if he would follow the same course of action.

"Launch fighters to protect the pods. The *Ro'arck* is to keep its position."

"But sir, they can't protect the pods as we can," wailed Satki.

"Follow orders or leave the bridge," he barked.

Satki nodded, wiping a tear from her eye.

"The enemy's primary weapon is sustaining damage," Drozah exclaimed. "Their shields are losing power."

Kaytrix observed his holo-screen with a thrill. Finally, some progress. Perhaps they weren't so invincible after all.

"They are moving off, Commander," Nat announced.

"Keep on them," he ordered, stalking the bridge while analyzing the holo-screens. He sensed they could prevail if they remained diligent. This Nevo ship appeared to have less dexterity for space combat.

Kersa gasped. "Sir, another Nevo vessel has appeared. It's directly behind us."

Shit. He should have anticipated this. "Position us behind the debris and use it as a shield," he said. "Bring up specs on the new ship from the sensors. I want to see what it has."

"Specs up," Kersa announced instantaneously.

"They are firing, sir!" Levro said.

The *Ro'arck* recoiled from a partial blast. Kaytrix fought to keep his footing as he skimmed the holographic information. This vessel had more power than the one they fought. It was faster too—a lot faster.

Another blast grazed the *Ro'arck* just as they took shelter behind the debris. The Varanus could still target them, but they were the least of Kaytrix's concerns. Thankfully, the Varanus fought among themselves while he tried to maneuver around his new predicament.

He glanced at the readings of the weakening Nevo vessel. It had lost power to its engines and now floated in space.

"Sir, the new enemy ship has destroyed all the pods. Squads 1 to 3 are falling fast," Levro said.

"Tell them to disengage the enemy and return to the ship," he said, watching his screen's blimps pulse and disappear. So, if the enemy couldn't attack him directly, they would try to draw him out? Clever.

The fighters continued to vanish. Only a handful boarded the *Ro'arck*. It was disturbing how quick men could lose their lives. He ground his teeth, the ache in his heart worsening. He would never use fighters again.

"Sir, the enemy is gaining on our position," Nat announced.

"I can't allow both ships to attack us. Position ourselves behind the weakened vessel. Let's see if they are cruel enough to kill their own to get to us."

Another blast flew through space toward them, but the projectile missed, hitting the weakening Nevo vessel instead. The shields rippled in protest. Kaytrix tried not to smile at their misfortune.

"Sir, our shields can regenerate given the time between the strikes, but I fear we can't play this game for much longer," Mac advised.

Indeed, it was a game. A dangerous game of seek and destroy. Kaytrix gazed back at his screen. The enemy's strength relied on distance to win. There were no short-range weapons on either of them. He could not win by hiding. It only prolonged the fight.

"Orders?" Levro inquired as they lingered in this brief stalemate.

Could they win this confrontation? There was no certainty in battle. "Prepare to engage thrusters. We will swing out and attack the weakened vessel and the long-range weapons of the other. Increase the shields in the forward section. Get ready. On my mark we will engage. Engage!"

The *Ro'arck* sped from beside the vessel, weapon batteries firing. They surprised the enemy, but it was short-lived.

Green weapons pelted the *Ro'arck* in furious blasts. The bombardment continued with unrelenting force.

"Our shields are failing, Commander," Mac said. "We can't keep this up much longer."

"Are we close to destroying their principal weapon?"

"Afraid not, sir."

Kaytrix ran a hand across his face. He hated the idea of leaving Varanus vulnerable to save their own skins, but the *Ro'arck's* shields were on the cusp of failure.

Another blast hit the *Ro'arck*, this time from the first enemy ship. The *Ro'arck* had maneuvered far enough away to be targeted by them.

"Orders, Commander?" Nat asked as she guided the *Ro'arck* around the second enemy ship.

"We can't take another blast," Mac announced. "Not if we want to live to fight another day."

Kaytrix reeled inside. They had no way of locating the enemy if they aborted. The idea of waiting for them to attack another valuable ally was not appealing. But what could they do? He only had a few moments to decide.

"Kaytrix, you know the marker drones we used to warn ships where black holes are?"

"Yeah?" he answered. Where was Mac going with this?

"I can reconfigure their programming so we can attach one to the enemy's hull and track it. Their pointed structure should theoretically penetrate the enemy shields, much like your blade, but I will need time to reprogram the subroutine."

"Hurry, Mac. We can't lose the *Ro'arck*. Nat, try to keep us beside this ship."

Mac left the bridge running.

Through the security cams, Kaytrix watched Mac rush to the engineering level. There he located the beacon drones, cozy in their storage. The *Ro'arck* shifted as Mac removed one's outer cover to expose the power crystals and the other components within.

Through the comm, Mac mumbled profanities. Mac was pushing himself, his fingers flying over the data pad with lightning speed.

Kaytrix returned his attention to the battle while Mac performed the task. He knew Mac enjoyed challenges, but this was a risky plan.

Another blast rocked the ship as Mac removed the crystal.

"Ah, drorse shit!" he said. "Try keeping the ship steadier, alright? I almost dropped the damn crystal."

"Hurry, Mac. The *Ro'arck* can't take very much more!" Kaytrix said.

"Yeah, don't I know it. I was at the damn terminal the whole time," Mac muttered to himself as he reinserted the reprogrammed crystal.

"Okay, I am ready," Mac said, reaching the hangar's center. "Launching the tracking beacon now."

Kaytrix spared a moment to watch Mac grapple with the odd remote. He stood piloting the drone through their hangar shields.

Kaytrix noted the weapons fire streaking past the opening and the looming enemy ship. He hoped the drone reached its destination without being destroyed first.

A moment passed. The *Ro'arck's* systems reached critical malfunction. Anticipation hung in the air as they waited. The second enemy ship approached, putting their plan at risk. They couldn't hide behind the other ship much longer. It was now or never.

"Kaytrix, the drone has landed! Mission accomplished!" Mac yelled into his comm.

"Nat, get us the hell out of here! Excellent work, Mac. Return to the bridge at once," Kaytrix said.

He monitored his screens as the *Ro'arck* distanced itself from the two ships, preparing to enter the portal. The second ship tore after them, firing massive amounts of energy their way in rapid succession. Many of the blasts passed over them, but not all would. He locked his jaw.

"Brace for impact!" he growled.

The *Ro'arck* made it through the portal but not before a blast struck the ship. Kaytrix flew forward into his command panel, his face hitting the solid surface. The taste of iron filled his mouth. Sparks flew from overhead bulkheads and broken light panels. The crew groaned and slowly recovered from the blast as they stood on their feet.

The stability of the bridge made it seem like the *Ro'arck* was in one piece, but a wailing alarm and a red holo-screen told him that wasn't the case.

Chapter 8

CONSEQUENCES

Kaytrix flipped through the *Ro'arck's* reports, discovering considerable damage to her sub-light engines. Thankfully, most of the other systems were still operational and not on the cusp of failure.

"Is everyone okay?" He gazed across the bridge and did a head count. Everyone seemed accounted for except . . . He activated his comm in his ear. "Mac, do you copy? Mac?"

There was a brief silence, then the comm emitted static.

"Yeah, yeah. I am here. Geesh. Don't get your knickers in a twist." Mac entered the bridge while peering down at a holographic screen, the bright orange revealing his smirk.

Kaytrix allowed himself a small smile and clasped Mac on the shoulder. "I thought you were a goner."

Mac looked at him, his eyes twinkling with mischief. "And what? Miss out on all this action? No way!" He strode to his station and began touching his screens.

Kaytrix did another visual check of the crew. He was glad they made it back in one piece, but he couldn't help feeling he could have done more for Varanus. Given the circumstances, he did more for them than the council had wanted.

The council. He wasn't looking forward to facing them and explaining why he had disobeyed orders. He hoped they would see the reasoning in his decision and not reprimand him for it.

The pulsing red holo-screen of the sub-light engines caught his attention. The *Narvent* was directly ahead.

"Can we dock, Nat?"

"I can, but I need to vent some atmosphere to control the ship. It's the only way I can bring us in." She looked back at him from her seat, the hint of a challenge in her tone.

"Very well."

Kaytrix fidgeted with his cape clasp. Watching Nat maneuver the ship the way she did brought out his nerves. How she could have such a powerful instinct for any ship she flew fascinated him. In a way, she shared a special language with the ship, knowing exactly how to get the desired results.

In moments they were docking, and he forced out the breath he'd been holding. No doubt the admiral was already aware of their return and awaiting his report. He rose from his seat and approached the sliding doors to the lift. He turned back to face Levro.

"I'll be back as soon as I can with our next mission, Lieutenant."

Levro saluted. "Yes, sir. I hope your report goes well." He returned to his tasks.

Me too, Kaytrix thought before he entered the lift.

⸻ ◈ ⸻

Standing before the council was taking its toll. They had read and reread his report, all while he stood there and waited. Occasionally, the council whispered with the admiral and glanced at him. It was unnerving. Were they mad? Disappointed? He wished they would get on with what they wanted to say.

Perseph sighed, irritated. Sarneft sat back in her chair, scowling, and Karva appeared deep in thought.

Ackon deactivated the report and peered at Kaytrix, his arms crossed. "To say I am surprised you disobeyed orders is an understatement," he huffed.

Kaytrix stood tall, determined to let him say his piece. His decision wasn't made lightly, and despite what the council thought, it was the right one to make.

"Even after we granted your request to have experienced crew board your vessel, this is how you thank us?" Sarneft spat.

He remained silent.

Karva looked across at Sarneft and the admiral. "Though we don't condone this behavior, we can see that Commander Torex's mission wasn't a failure."

"Really?" Perseph snorted. He rose from the table to prowl around Kaytrix. "The results of the Varanus turmoil could very well have set us back. If this faction of rebels believes the Nevo can deliver them greatness for abandoning us, they will fight for it. The Nevo could have already taken over Varanus and are preparing further invasions."

The admiral held his chin thoughtfully. "Yes, that is true. But we can deal with a Varanus skirmish easier if we can locate and destroy this Nevo influence." The admiral looked from Perseph to Kaytrix. "Commander, your decision to disobey orders will not go unpunished. However, since you have implemented a way to track the enemy, I am ordering you to seek them out once the repairs on the *Ro'arck* are complete."

"Yes, sir." He released some tension he'd been holding in his jaw, but the admiral wasn't done speaking.

"As for your punishment, we are withholding a full solar rotation of earnings."

Kaytrix's heart stopped, a deepening pain sinking into his chest. "Admiral, my ma is sick. Without my earnings—"

"You should have thought of that before you disobeyed the orders of the council," Perseph interjected.

Kaytrix refused to look at Perseph. If he did, the desire to punch his lights out would be too great, councillor or not. Instead, he forced out the breath he'd been holding.

"Yes, sir."

The admiral stood from his place at the table. "That is all, Commander Torex."

Kaytrix saluted and left the inner chambers. He hadn't considered that they would take an entire solar rotation's worth of pieces. How was his father supposed to take care of his ma if he couldn't pay for her medicine?

He entered the lift and selected the level for the arkross. A feeling of foolishness overcame him. He shouldn't have disobeyed his orders. Instead of only him being punished for his actions, his parents would also suffer. It didn't make sense. A lot of things didn't. Like the information he had copied from the archive and the heated conversation he had overheard. He wanted to know what had been happening on O'ber before he got there and why the council wanted to keep the allies out of this conflict.

Kaytrix walked across the access corridor from the *Narvent* to the *Ro'arck* when an idea struck him. Without Mac, he could have never turned a drone into a locator beacon. Maybe Mac would look at the files and decode them?

Kaytrix entered the *Ro'arck* and found Mac squatted behind his terminal, working on the crystals and their arrangement within the tray. His frazzled red hair caught the light of the console, evidence he'd stoked it a few times.

"Hey, Mac, do you have a second?"

His friend bit the tip of his tongue in concentration. "That all depends on how nice you ask me." He smirked.

Kaytrix regarded Mac's yellowing teeth and shrunk back from his old breath. "Ahem, well, since I'm your commanding officer, you don't have a choice."

Mac rose to pull his britches up, shaking his head at Kaytrix as he closed the tray of crystals. "You're going to use that card on me, eh? Fine, fine. I'm done here anyway. What do you need?"

Kaytrix observed as the rest of the bridge crew carried on with their tasks of maintenance and system reboots. Before talking with Mac, he should see how the repairs were going. He held up a finger. "Hold that thought."

Mac rolled his eyes and crossed his arms. "Sure, sure," he said.

"Lieutenant, report on the repairs?"

Levro brought over a portable holographic display. The bright blue colors shone on his uniform, canceling out the grays.

"Sir, the repairs are 50 percent complete. The *Narvent* crew are working quickly and project to be finished come the beginning of tomorrow." He touched the display. "The main damage on the sub-light engines is taking the most time."

Kaytrix held his chin. Would that be enough time for Mac to work his magic on the coded files from the archive? It was worth a shot.

"Thank you, Lieutenant. As you were."

Once Levro had walked away, Kaytrix turned to Mac, who had resorted to twisting his beard while he waited for him.

"Ready?" Kaytrix asked when he caught Nat looking his way, an eyebrow arched. There was no reason he couldn't involve her or Drozah in this truth. In fact, it might take some of the burden off him, but he had to be careful. He didn't want his decisions affecting their careers. He motioned her over and indicated for her to bring Drozah.

"Yes, Commander?" Nat asked, folding her arms behind her back.

"Let's take a walk," he motioned for them to follow. He led them to his quarters and closed the door behind them.

"What's this all about?" Drozah asked, his form rigid, defensive.

"Relax, you're not in trouble," Kaytrix reassured him. "I have something to share with you, but before you listen to it, I need to know if you are willing to risk your careers."

Mac shrugged. "I'm in."

Nat was silent, but Drozah shifted his weight uncomfortably. "Kaytrix, I know we're friends and I support you, but I have a young family. I don't know what this is, but if it risks their safety, I'm out," rumbled Drozah.

Kaytrix saluted him. "Thank you for your honesty, Drozah."

Drozah nodded and exited the room, leaving the small space feeling empty.

"And you?" Kaytrix asked, looking at Nat.

She was scrutinizing him, no doubt weighing her loyalty to her passion and to him as a friend. Finally, she said, "I can't decide without knowing all the information, Kaytrix. You know that isn't fair."

"You are right." He rocked on his heels. Could he risk this secret with his friends? "Alright, I'll tell you, then you can decide."

He told them the story of O'ber, the concerns the council had shared on their resources being drained to a war, and what he had found in the archives. He shared his suspicions of the council hiding something, and how he needed Mac's help to decode the files if he could.

Nat scowled. Had he made a mistake in telling her?

"Kaytrix, I've known you for a long time, and I don't know what's happened in the last ten solar rotations . . ."

Regret settled into his bones, but he kept a calm composure, allowing her to finish.

"I'm not totally against what you are saying you witnessed, but I can't turn my back on the council, either." She crumpled her brow. "I never thought you would question the council."

He threw his hands up. "I am only asking you to hear me out, to see if what I am suspecting is true or not. If this fight has been going on for that long, why are we just learning of it now?"

Mac cracked his neck, breaking the tension between them. "I say, if they have nothing to hide, the files wouldn't require an access code," he said.

Nat's form relaxed. "You're right, Mac. Okay, Kaytrix, you have a point. If they *are* hiding something, what are you going to do about it?"

The question caught him off guard. "I don't know, but I'll think of something."

She nodded toward Mac. "Think you can crack the toughest code in all the galaxy?"

Mac rolled his eyes, bending his fingers forward to crack his knuckles. "Natty, I was born to make and break codes."

"You will do it then?" Kaytrix asked. He couldn't believe his luck.

Mac nodded and pointed to his gauntlet. "I'll copy the information and get started on it right away, but I can't guarantee when I will have it completed."

Kaytrix nodded. Of course, he didn't expect miracles. "I understand. Now let's get back to the bridge. The crew doesn't know about this, and I'd like to keep this between us."

"I will seal my lips," Nat said, motioning with her hand over her mouth. "I'll see you both out there." She saluted and left the room.

Memories of their past together at the academy surfaced. All the chances Kaytrix had to say something about his feelings were turning into regrets.

Mac slapped him on the shoulder. "When are you going to ask her out? It's killing me and Drozah to see you skirting around your feelings. That, and we have a bet to settle." He winked.

Kaytrix gave him a friendly shove. "Too much time has passed. We're not graduates anymore. Besides, I am sure she's got someone else in her life."

Mac shook his head as he started copying the files. "You give up too easy."

Kaytrix sighed. Maybe Mac was right. Once this was all over, he would make a point of addressing his feelings for her.

Chapter 9

AMBUSH

Kaytrix stood alone on the command deck, watching the *Narvent* maintenance droids travel up and down the hull, finishing with the last of the repairs.

The bridge was dark, the only light coming from the various holo-screens in sleep mode. The crew were asleep in their quarters and so the starship floated in a slumber. He would also rest if so much didn't weigh on his mind.

Before turning in for the night, Mac had informed him that the locator beacon they planted was giving off a strong signal and the file decoding was underway. Kaytrix laid awake, thinking of what the contents of the archive would reveal, but also the cost his decisions would have on his family.

As much as he wanted to tell his family about the loss of his wages, he didn't have the heart. News like that was better left for in person. He hoped he would have time to see them again.

"Couldn't sleep?"

The voice startled him. He turned to see Nat, her silhouette defined by a dim light behind her.

"Seems you couldn't either." He resumed watching the droids work. He could hear her soft footfalls on the smooth deck floor as she approached.

"Pretty hard to. Lots on my mind with this war. Why wouldn't the council tell us about the Nevo? We could have ended this skirmish if everyone had known."

Kaytrix turned to look into her soft brown eyes. "That's what I can't wrap my mind around." His eyes lingered on the soft features of her face before looking away. She could always make his heart warm, no matter the context of their conversation.

She laid a hand on his forearm. "I can't imagine it was easy bearing this secret, but you have us to support you, Kaytrix."

He laughed. "You mean like the time you had me lie to your parents about where you were so you could spend time with that older Warrior clan graduate? What was his name? Oh yes, *Ryke*." He said the name in a mocking tone, remembering being jealous of Ryke's Warrior clan status and the fact that Nat found him attractive.

Nat punched his arm playfully. "That's not the same!" she insisted. "Besides, I still appreciate you covering for me. And that night, Ryke showed his true colors. If it weren't for you, I wouldn't have learned how much of a jerk he could be."

She smiled at him, and his cheeks flushed. He looked at her round nose, and then her lips. She was so close, her flowery scent suddenly the only thing his brain could register . . .

Buzz, buzz. The comm in his inner ear rattled, snapping him out of the moment.

"Commander Torex here," he answered.

"Commander," came Zilas's voice from the *Narvent*. "The repairs to the *Ro'arck* are complete. I have also outfitted the *Ro'arck* with a modified weapon based on your experience fighting the enemy on O'ber. You have six missiles retrofitted with a sharp end, designed to penetrate shielding and then explode."

"Thank you, Zilas. Commander Torex out."

Nat studied his face expectantly.

"Time to wake the crew," he said.

In moments, the crew were at their stations and the *Ro'arck* was departing from her port at the station. The crew appeared rested, though he was sure they were tired of the rude awakenings in the early hours of the morning.

"Awaiting coordinates for the beacon to be added to the navigations terminal," Levro announced.

From the forward section of the bridge, Nat called, "Coordinates received and locked. We are ready to initiate jump sequence."

Kaytrix calmed a shiver traveling through his back. What would the Nevo ships think of their sudden appearance?

"Alright, crew, we may only get one shot at this, so listen up." He stood from his seat and paced the bridge. "We know one ship has severe damage. We will target it first. If the second ship is around, we will use the same tactic as before, using it as a barrier to their long-range weapons. We have six new missiles to use against them. Try to make them count."

"Yes, sir!" the crew members called in unison.

He sat back down. "Activate shields and engage the jump."

A large portal opened before them in hues of purple and blue, its swirling energy resembling a hurricane. The *Ro'arck* proceeded through, arriving on the other side where it was dark and void of any planets, with remnants of solar winds and gases from sister solar systems.

"We have a signal coming from the tracking drone, sir," reported Levro. "I am not detecting any Nevo ships. They must have discovered the drone and discarded it."

Kaytrix stared out into the dark. A feeling of being watched crept into his mind—the same feeling he had experienced at O'ber. The enemy could be anywhere, signals detected or not.

"Let's try to retrieve the drone, Mac," he said, watching his friend leave the bridge deck at a run. "Everyone keep alert," he warned, pacing.

They neared the drone's location without Analyst Officer Kersa announcing detections. Had the Nevo dropped the drone and retreated?

"I'm at the hanger," came Mac's voice through the comm. "Attempting to pilot the drone back."

"Affirmative, Mac. Be careful." Kaytrix continued to stare at the space before him, puzzling at the odd scenario when the answer struck him. His realization came too late as two Nevo ships appeared out of the interstellar medium.

"It's an ambush! Evasive maneuvers. Target the damaged ship and fire our new missiles!" Kaytrix barked.

The *Ro'arck* dove, missing the blasts, and sped into a cloud of gas. Nat positioned them behind the enemy in the perfect firing zone. This was the moment to see if they were right about the shielding.

"Fire!"

Multiple crossed-end missiles tore from their gun ports, streaking a trail of red. They spun toward the enemy at a bold speed, meeting their mark in mere seconds. There was a pulse of green across the enemy vessel and Kaytrix's heart sank. Were these missiles also ineffective? Kaytrix almost looked away when an explosion within the shield raked the surface of the Nevo ship.

"Direct hit, Commander!" Drozah said. "We got through their shields, but their hull is durable. It's going to take a few more missiles!"

A surge of adrenaline rushed through him. "Get another attack lined up. We can't waste this opportunity. What's the damage on the other vessel?" Kaytrix demanded. His eyes dared not leave the battlefield.

"Minimal damage, sir. It has broken formation with the damaged ship," reported Lieutenant Levro.

"Focus fire on the weakening ship. Let's finish this," Kaytrix growled.

Plasma from their guns whizzed through space and struck the ship. They pressed their attack and the Nevo vessel slowed, losing power. A ripple effect of sparks soon crawled along the enemy ship's surface, signaling shield failure. The *Ro'arck's* weapons penetrated deeper into the enemy's hull, triggering multiple overloads. The vessel's hull collapsed, surrendering to the power of their weapons.

Kaytrix sensed an inevitable victory.

The damaged ship came to a stop as flame built, caged within the ship's skeleton. A raging inferno consumed the oxygen and gushed between the weakened structure and beyond the failing shield. The explosion tore the Nevo ship apart.

The *Ro'arck* swayed from the blast. A surge of victory radiated throughout Kaytrix's chest. They had destroyed the ship. Such an accomplishment was long overdue, but in their minor victory, one threat remained.

"What's the status of the remaining ship?" he demanded.

"The other vessel has intensified their attack on us, sir," reported Kersa. "It appears we have angered them."

Kaytrix allowed himself a sneer. After all the Archarian lives they lost, he found it satisfying for the enemy to taste the same effects of battle.

"Our shields won't last much longer at this rate, Commander," Levro shouted as warnings drowned the bridge with screams.

"Nat, can you get us out of their range? Or get us closer?"

"I can't get away from him!" she called.

Sweat trickled down Kaytrix's brow. He had seconds before their shields overloaded and they lost their ship. He rushed through his options when the bombardment ceased.

"Commander," Satki announced abruptly. "They are hailing us."

The announcement caught him by surprise, and a wave of apprehension overtook him. Was he ready to see the face of his adversary?

"Make sure nothing tries to sneak up behind us," he advised, resuming his place in the command chair. "Open the channel," he said, clearing his throat.

He fidgeted with his cape clasp while waiting for the connection. He wasn't sure what to expect. Would they look the same as the soldier he had encountered on O'ber, with the glaring green eyes?

Communications Officer Satki pressed a sequence of buttons and a hologram appeared before the commander, its likeness something Kaytrix had never seen before, not even at O'ber. Intense glaring eyes penetrated the darkness and the space between them. A face of black metal with green streaks met his gaze. Horizontal fangs protruded beside a grated mouth in a head that came to a sharp point. Slivers of green skin showed through cracks in the metal, as if melted to each other. Jagged edges pointed from the alien's shoulders where a dark cape draped over its body.

A chill ran through Kaytrix's spine as a large dagger-like finger pointed at him.

"So," a sibilant voice breathed. "You are the one responsible for the annihilation of my ship."

Each word crawled over Kaytrix's skin. He feared the grating voice would dominate his nightmares.

"Identify yourself," he demanded.

There was a hesitation, as if his request startled his opponent. Or was he being scrutinized?

Dim light flashed from the enemy's eyes, as if they were angry. "I am Lord Khelveliz of the Nevo. Leader of my planet, O'ber. Who are *you*?"

A chill traveled the nape of Kaytrix's neck as he swallowed past a lump. "I am Commander Kaytrix Torex of the Archarian vessel, the *Ro'arck*."

There was another pause. A flash of green emitted from the Nevo's eyes, followed by a hiss. What did that information mean to this strange entity? Had Kaytrix made a mistake in identifying himself?

"Commander Torex," the Nevo lord spoke again, stressing the pronunciation. "I have plans of revenge and your pathetic skin insists on challenging me."

Kaytrix's temper threatened his composure. "Your presence in the galaxy is unwelcome. Today proved we can fight against you and win. I suggest you leave while you can," he warned.

The holographic silhouette of Lord Khelveliz stared blankly at him, as if his words meant nothing. "Oh, I don't plan to go anywhere, *Archarian*. My revenge involves your world and its complete annihilation."

Fear twisted Kaytrix's insides. "Not as long as I am breathing, *Khelveliz*," he said, forcing himself to speak. He hoped his show of bravery was enough to outweigh his growing panic.

Lord Khelveliz laughed a hearty, gross laugh. "Well," he said. "If that is the *only* thing standing in my way, then I shall kill you."

Kaytrix swallowed past a lump forming in his throat. "The worlds within the alliance are under our protection," he growled.

The Nevo's eyes glared viciously. "Time will tell, Commander Torex. Even as we speak, worlds are being overthrown by my newly acquired armies."

Kaytrix's throat tightened as flashes of O'ber resurfaced. The memory of being strangled made him reel. Lord Khelveliz's words seeped through the hologram and latched onto him, causing a sudden darkness to swell within him. His soul felt invaded.

With a swift punch to his console, Kaytrix ended the transmission and gasped as if released from an invisible grip. The Nevo lord's claims stunned him. There was no way they could be true.

"He's opening fire!" Levro announced.

Nat swerved the *Ro'arck* to avoid the blast, but they took the full force of the hit. Wails and red light drowned the bridge in an ominous mood.

"Don't let him escape!" Kaytrix ordered. "Fire the new missiles!"

Drozah opened fire, but Lord Khelveliz's ship dodged the attack with ease and disappeared through a portal.

"Ugh!" Kaytrix fumed. "Is there any way to know where he went?"

"No, sir, I am afraid not," Kersa said.

He slammed a fist on his armrest. "Dammit!" This would have been a perfect opportunity to end all their problems. If only their shields were stronger.

"Orders, sir?" Levro asked.

He let his anger simmer for a moment. "Where were we hit?" he asked, glancing to his screen. Multiple reports poured in, making it impossible to find the information he sought.

"Sir, the blast caught us on an angle just as we tried to avoid it hitting our port side. It severely damaged the hangar," Levro said. "There are multiple fire alerts throughout the surrounding corridors."

Kaytrix gazed at Levro, a knot twisting in his stomach. Mac should have returned by now. "Take us home, Lieutenant. Have emergency crews put the fires out. Then dock with the *Narvent*. Have their repair crews start at once," he ordered.

"Where are you going, sir?"

"To find Mac."

He abandoned the bridge and headed for the hangar, pulling on a respirator. He tried calling Mac again. There was no response. He breathed slow through his respirator, trying to remain calm. Now was not the time to choke on his air supply. Mac was probably busy helping other crew members.

The lift opened to the hangar's level. Dark marks from fire streaked the corridor. Crew caught in the explosion lay scattered, their bodies locked in their last moments of escape. Nausea settled in his stomach. He forced the bile down as he stepped over the bodies. So far, this wasn't looking good.

He activated the comm in his inner ear. "Medical teams to the hangar at once." Further along he came upon a crew member caught in the blaze. Despite Kaytrix's queasiness, he knelt to brace the fallen crew member against the ship's passage wall.

An intersecting corridor shielded the man from the full force of the fire, but it had not saved him from the brutality of the heat. The folds of skin hid his eyes as he struggled to breathe.

Kaytrix tried not to make eye contact as he sprayed a healing disinfectant agent on the man's face. It would stop the spread of the burn, but this man needed more than spray to heal his wounds.

The man reached out and laid a hand on Kaytrix's forearm. "Kill me," the man begged.

The plea froze Kaytrix, or was it the layers of skin falling from the man's hand? He swallowed. "Help is on the way," he said, trying to sound reassuring. He rose and continued to the hangar.

After that encounter, he feared the worst for Mac. He wished he hadn't sent him to retrieve the drone. He navigated through the damaged sections, avoiding looking at the bodies. Upon arriving at the hangar, his heart sank. He could hardly recognize it.

Parts of the *Ro'arck* melted in on itself while fighter ships lay scattered, aflame. Pilots' bodies littered the floor. The intense heat shrunk their muscles and flexed their joints, contorting them into pugilistic poses.

From a glance, he could tell that the attack penetrated their shields, striking the very edge of the hanger. It was enough to cause extensive damage and ignite the shuttle's power source, causing a chain reaction. That led to the fire spreading past the doors and through the corridors.

Kaytrix's heart sank as he recognized a tuft of red hair on a body off to the side.

"Mac . . ." he said, falling to his knees. He gazed upon the thin, charred face of his friend. He sobbed silently, clenching his fists. Regret settled into his bones. His friend was dead, and it was his fault.

Chapter 10

ENTRAPMENT

Kaytrix reported to the council. It was nighttime on Archaria, and the lit candles and dim lights did little to soothe the darkness within. Standing before them in the great round room, he reported the events of his mission in detail. He found it difficult keeping his composure. Everything from the accident still raw and fresh.

He finished reiterating his report and waited. Now the council knew their enemy's name, Lord Khelveliz, and his intentions for his attacks on their alliance and their ships. Through all the pain Kaytrix was dealing with, he hoped the council would bring the alliance into the fight. That way the mission wouldn't be a failure, and Mac's death hadn't been for nothing.

Perseph rose from his seat and shook his finger at Kaytrix. "I knew this was a waste of time!" He turned to the other council members and the admiral. "And if you had listened to me in the first place, we would be better off. This Lord Khelveliz now has armies, and our delay in taking the arkross has doomed all our efforts!"

Sarneft stood to glare at him. "Sit down, Perseph. Plans are still in motion. Today is the day we harvest the fruits of our labor."

Perseph crossed his arms.

Sarneft continued to stare him down, her aged eyes like daggers. "Sit."

Perseph finally sat.

Kaytrix's skin crawled. Plans. More like schemes. And what exactly were those schemes? A wave of emotion washed over him as he remembered

Mac. Not only had he lost a life-long friend, but now the archive files would forever remain coded. He tried to avoid thinking of his friend, but it was difficult. He hadn't mourned his death.

Losing his friend and many other Archarian soldiers weighed on his mind. He was exhausted. Mac's death was another chisel to his resolve as a soldier and a leader.

His hands shook. Was it better that he didn't know what the council was up to? The more he questioned everything around him, the more people he cared about suffered. He couldn't take any more losses.

"Commander." Ackon drew in a breath. "I am disappointed in you."

The words hit Kaytrix hard. "Sir?"

"Your inability to follow orders has put the alliance in jeopardy. Because of your choices, the Varanus have maintained their ability to infiltrate other worlds at a rate that we cannot sustain, led by this Nevo lord," Ackon said, his tone harsh.

Kaytrix's jaw tightened, and his anger bubbled. "With all due respect, sir, we know more about the enemy now than before. We can fight and win."

Ackon shook his head. "That no longer matters, Commander."

Kaytrix's eyebrow twitched as he tried to make sense of the admiral's words. The council members' faces were expectant. Perseph appeared more smug than usual. Did he enjoy his frustration?

"Commander, so far in your commanding position, your recklessness has cost us thousands of Archarian lives and wasted valuable resources, putting us in jeopardy with the rise of this new threat." Perseph sneered.

Kaytrix glowered at Perseph. Now he understood more of the council's true intentions of giving him the *Ro'arck* to command. They needed a scapegoat, someone to take the blame for all their mistakes in managing this conflict, and he was the perfect candidate. No one would question their decisions due to their position. It was easier to believe the Farmer-turned-Warrior had made a mistake.

Kaytrix fought his anger, controlling his tone. He couldn't believe they were trying to peg this on him! "This war isn't just starting, is it? It's a century in the making." How could they blame him for using precious resources? "Whatever your schemes are, it is costing Archaria. I have witnessed the repercussions of *your* poor—"

"Enough!" Perseph said. "We really should thank you for all you've done, Commander. Without you, none of this would be possible."

Kaytrix bristled at the comment. "I stand by my decision to support Varanus. Can you say the same for all the decisions you've made, Councillor?"

Sarneft rose to speak, her robes flying with the motion. "You are not to insinuate anything against us, Commander. We have evidence of your treachery to Archaria. You are to be arrested and tried accordingly."

Kaytrix glanced over at each of them. He focused on Karva, the councillor who defied the others' plans earlier. Though he stood in a room of darkness, one light shone at the end of his tunnel. All he had to do was reach.

"Regardless of the *evidence* you have against me, if you wait to inform the allies of this war, it *will* be too late. For all of us," he said.

Sarneft's nostrils flared, her eyes wild. "The allies are convening with us in several rotations when they will learn that you are the reason for all of this: lost lives, lost resources, lost ships. Your ability to join us has played a vital role in maintaining the image of Archaria. Congratulations, soldier, you have served your purpose."

He couldn't believe the lies they bought into, lies they spun for themselves. How was maintaining the image of Archaria more important than the planet itself and its people?

"Time to go," Sarneft spat. She raised her hand, signaling the imperial guards. "You are to be imprisoned until a proper hearing can commence."

In his peripheral vision, there was movement. Several imperial guards approached from either side and from behind him. His blood boiled, the collar of his armor tightening as his rage swelled.

Sarneft sneered. "Take him away," she ordered.

His body went rigid in preparation to resist the guards. All this time, he had wanted to believe the council had the people's interest at heart. Now he knew the truth. He hated the idea of watching from a prison cell as his beloved planet fell into ruin.

He tried thinking of a plan. The imperial guards' footsteps were closer now.

If he wanted to change the council's choices, he had to put them in a predicament. He recalled what Ackon had said several rotations earlier. If their people learned of this confrontation, it could create mass hysteria. That was it! He could use evidence of the council's dishonesty as leverage. If the council refused to involve the allies, he would broadcast the truth to all the cities of Archaria.

Anxiety swelled in his chest as he summoned the courage to speak. If they suspected his bluff, they could imprison him for life—or worse, sentence his parents for being accomplices. Whatever happened in this moment, there was no room in his heart for the deceitful ways of the council. He'd had enough. The time to act was now, before men needlessly lost their lives, before he was locked up forever.

He raised his hands. "Wait," he demanded, surprised when the guards listened. "I have something to say before you take me away."

Sarneft rose her eyebrows as she settled in her seat. "I'll entertain your words. Speak," she snarled.

"I have successfully decoded thousands of files from the archive regarding O'ber and the Nevo. I have downloaded them to the broadcasting satellite of the *Narvent*, ready to be televised the moment I press this button. If you try to frame me for crimes I have not committed, Archaria and the alliance will learn the truth of your deception."

The councillors' faces melted into horror as he poised his hand above his gauntlet.

Ackon's face beaded with sweat, his hands tightening into fists on the marble table.

Perseph looked impressed but not amused.

Sarneft glowered at his brazenness.

Karva's face was blank, tears threatening the threshold of his eyes.

Kaytrix waited, sensing the guards' confusion.

"You're clever for a farm boy, but something tells me you aren't that intelligent to pull this off," Perseph spat, twirling his hair with a spindly finger.

"I should thank you for sending Mac Secu to join me on the *Ro'arck*," Kaytrix countered, resisting the impulse to laugh at Perseph's shocked expression. Kaytrix directed his attention to the shattering composure of Karva Norda. What would happen now?

Sarneft shot from her seat. "He's lying! Take him away!" she spat, pointing a knobby finger at him.

Kaytrix lowered his finger as the guards stepped closer.

"NO!" Karva stood, waving his hands.

"Are you out of your mind?" Sarneft growled, her eyes darting to Karva.

"We can't let the people find out this way!" Karva yelled.

"You're weak," she hissed.

"And you are afraid to admit the truth," Karva retorted.

His insult seemed to cut through Sarneft, and she stared at him. The guards remained poised and ready. The clan representatives burst into arguments with the admiral on what to do. It was as if Kaytrix's threat poisoned their minds. The Great Hall they stood in, once filled with the quiet murmurs of peace talks of their ancestors, now echoed with chaos. The leaders of the Archarian democracy argued and insulted each other. Their rage escalated into a wild frenzy of shouts, wearing his tolerance raw.

"Enough!" Kaytrix called out, slamming his fist onto the stone table before him.

The council ceased yelling at once, their focus on his sudden act of violence in their presence.

He withdrew his fist. "Arguing will not solve the issue at hand. We must gather our forces and call on the allies for help before the enemy attacks again."

"You have no business ordering us around," Sarneft fumed, her aged eyes piercing his soul.

"I serve Archaria and everyone who lives in our region," he said. "It is my job to serve a truthful, peaceful council with integrity. None of you display those qualities. So, let's start off with honesty. What happened in the O'ber system on missions 3199 and 3200? Why do they date from a century prior? Why are they blank in the archives?"

"Shouldn't you know that?" Sarneft mocked, looking away. It seemed obvious Kaytrix's presence was more than a nuisance.

Karva Norda coughed. "The commander is right. We need to come clean if we have any hopes of making this right."

Grumbles passed between the members and the admiral as they sat, their tempers cooling.

"Telling him will do little good and expose mistakes. The first mistake being that clan members should not take on roles besides the ones they are born to," Perseph complained, his eyes darting from Karva to Kaytrix. He had abandoned his hair to twirl what little beard existed on his chin. "Your clan belongs in the fields. Otherwise you make mistakes. Just like Karva here . . ."

Kaytrix's patience waned as he clenched his jaw, resisting the urge to comment. One thing was certain—he was better suited for the battlefield or farming. Anything but backstabbing politics.

"Mistakes or not, working with Commander Torex is in our best interest," Karva spoke again. He uncrossed his arms. "Archaria cannot be in chaos while a war rages on in the galaxy. If we are going to fight, it should be against this enemy, not each other."

Perseph lowered his eyes but remained scowling.

Sarneft crossed her arms, her silence an agreement to Karva's point.

Kaytrix drew in a quick breath. This was taking too long, but it had to run its course.

Karva cleared his throat and settled into his chair. The dim light from the various lights and candles aged his face significantly. "Mission 3199 was one mistake after another," he said. "Archaria lost a recon ship in the O'ber system, and the council gave permission for a rescue team to retrieve the ship. As soon as they landed on the foreign soil, someone attacked. Only one Archarian returned from that mission."

"What happened?" Kaytrix asked.

Karva blinked as if trying to refresh a memory. "A symbiotic race inhabited the planet. We believe that before we arrived, they had no technological advancements. Based on the report of the survivor, and the blade you submitted, we've confirmed this race survives inside other life forms. Their intelligence is limited to their hosts' . . ." Karva's voice wavered, growing grave. "They fortify their bodies with metal to prevent deterioration. Often they have entire body parts removed and fitted with mechanical ones."

Kaytrix swallowed, remembering the soldier on O'ber.

The councillors' eyes hollowed with failure and contempt.

Kaytrix rehashed the councillor's words. "Wait . . . You're not saying . . . *We* caused this?" he asked, his knees feeling weak.

"We lost more than the lives of my men," Karva admitted, a single tear rolling down his sagging cheeks. "We lost the knowledge of the Archarian race. Everything that made us who we are—our secrets, our allies, our weaknesses . . . stolen and distorted."

The information was hard to accept. They created this enemy! But why would Lord Khelveliz have such a hatred for them? Something wasn't adding up.

"Wait? *Your* men?" Kaytrix did the math. "So, this did happen 110 solar rotations ago!" He couldn't believe they had kept this a secret for so long. This war had raged on for many solar rotations, sucking the life out of Archaria's resources. Was that why they refused to call the allies? Were they embarrassed to admit the enemy they fought they inadvertently created?

Karva raised his gaze to the commander, his eyes old, weak, and frail with the responsibility he bore on his shoulders. "I am the sole survivor. Like you, I was young, and from the Farmer clan. Fear kept me from leaving the ship, and I let my squad become the enemy. After the incident, I joined the council to clean up the mess we made, but also to preserve the truth."

Kaytrix opened his mouth to speak, but he couldn't find the words to say. Not only had they kept this deadly truth a secret, but their enemy had drained their resources and was now turning their allies against them. This was worse than he ever imagined.

The aged councillor wiped his cheek. "How do we face their power, Commander? We've exhausted our resources," Karva said hopelessly.

"Not every resource," Kaytrix stated. "They aren't invincible. Our improved missiles prove that, but we can't expect to win this alone."

"You can't involve the allies. They and the nations of Archaria can't know what we have done. What we have tried to preserve," Karva pleaded.

"Exposing the truth will ruin all of us," Ackon said.

Kaytrix's anger rose to the surface. He hadn't forgotten what they had tried to do. "You should have thought about that before," he growled. "My concern right now is to succeed against Lord Khelveliz. The truth will reveal itself when it is time, and when it does, the people will handle you."

"Then we will inform the allies what has transpired," Ackon said, folding his hands together.

"We will do what you ask, as long as you don't share the files." Karva swallowed, wiping another tear away.

Kaytrix observed their sweaty, privileged, worried faces. He owed them nothing. What they had tried to do was barbaric and shameful. As much as he wanted to expose them, he couldn't with a bluff.

"Yes, and I will no longer cover for mistakes committed by the council," he said.

Karva nodded, folding his arms within the cuffs of his black tunic. "Very well. We will discuss their ability to help us as soon as possible. Don't release the files."

Kaytrix almost promised he wouldn't, but his parents still suffered without his pay. "I will on another condition."

Perseph sighed and rolled his eyes. "What now? An empire for yourself?"

"The release of my earnings," he growled. "That way my ma can carry on with her medication."

"Done," Ackon said and immediately typed on his holo-screen.

Perseph and Sarneft grumbled, their faces a testament to what they were thinking. It was obvious they were livid at his way of forcing their hand and ruining their plans. Now they had no choice but to cooperate and take orders from him.

Oh, how the tables had turned.

Chapter 11

THE ALLIANCE

Kaytrix stood in the dim command center, bracing his arm and holding his chin. As much as he was eager to board the *Ro'arck* and escape the council's hypocrisy, the councillors needed him here with the admiral and vice admirals.

He forced his physical and mental exhaustion away and attempted to coordinate with the admiral on fleet placement. It was awkward at first. The admiral never said much, only mumbled under his breath. The vice admirals ignored him completely, which was fine. The less opinions, the more productive they could be. He understood that their reluctance was because of his actions, but as rotations passed, the admiral shed his dismissive self and became relaxed.

Kaytrix stood beside the admiral as they delegated their fleet to important sectors, ensuring that experienced commanders paired with the less experienced. They agreed to create as many shield-piercing missiles as they could and install them on their starships.

It was a promising idea in theory, but already, several rotations in, the process was slow. Even with their production on the planet Konsuia, their primary ship and weapons' builder, missiles were taking longer than expected.

Kaytrix exhaled and touched the holographic screen. The blue grid displayed their fleets across the galaxy.

"I'm not sure this is going to be enough." He combed his hair back with his hand. "Even with the missiles and our ships, I've seen what Lord

Khelveliz can do. It would take a blockade of ships to prevent him from tearing through our defenses."

The admiral crossed his arms. "You're saying we're spread too thin?" he huffed.

Kaytrix leaned on the projection platform. "I'm saying we may need to ask our allies for more help."

The admiral was mid-sentence when an imperial guard entered the room and saluted. The clash of his fist on his armor drew their attention.

"Admiral, the allies are arriving through the arkross. They're on their way to the council chambers."

"Thank you." The admiral returned the salute, his face thoughtful. "You and I best be a part of this, Commander Torex. I can't imagine the news will impress them. You go on ahead and I will catch up after finishing here."

Kaytrix nodded, thankful for a moment to step out. The last few rotations had been stressful, from bluffing the council to preparing the fleet. He hadn't been back to the *Ro'arck* since his return from the mission and still grieved for Mac. He'd received several updates about the status of the *Ro'arck's* repairs and was grateful, but it burdened him he couldn't see Nat or Drozah while mourning their friend.

Levro had mentioned while repairs were underway that he, Nat, and Tuce were trying to devise a way to detect the enemy's unique sub-light engine energy. Every ship left a trail of exhausted energy. The *Ro'arck's* sensors had detected it a few times, enabling them to replicate and synthesize a way to search it out. It would prove handy if they could get it working; it would prevent Lord Khelveliz from fleeing again.

Kaytrix ran a hand over his face as he exited the command center. He couldn't remember the last time he was this tired. As he neared the lift, various members of the alliance left the arkross room. He paused. Who had arrived?

The first was Larx Tarknic, leader of the Shrovons, a humanoid race who excelled in melee and held honor as their highest possession. Then the King of Cordabo, Saielis Shad, a mighty man whose race prided themselves on knowledge and technological advancements through experimentation and science. Beside him was the Hossin representative, Rix Varkors, waltzing in proudly, his muzzle held high. His race curated some of the finest foods and beverages in the land and hosted some amazing celebrations on their agriculturally rich world.

Farther behind was the chief of Zaguarz, Chief Kovex. He strode in with a limp, and new scars across his face. A stab of pain shot through Kaytrix. He wished he would have found out more about what happened to the chief's merchant ship and his planet.

Beside the chief strode T'res K'netch, leader of the Drovons. The soot on his clothes and gray fur did little to dull the sharpness of his pristine canine eyes. The Drovon race were known for their ability to forge any material into a useful object, making them formidable allies.

They boarded the lift and after a moment it returned empty just in time to receive Beto B'vel, the Konsuian representative. One could never guess by his compact frame that his race possessed the most sophisticated weapons production facilities in the area.

Kaytrix caught his breath. A being rarely seen entered the Grand Tower: Queen Rayla of the Shargans, and her personal guard, T'vos. She walked past him, smiling. The cells in his body buzzed. Since she was a being of pure energy, he was sure she had that effect on many.

The Shargan race was older than the Archarians and possessed powerful abilities that could shift this war into their favor. The queen of the Shargans was the most powerful of all, more powerful than one of their finest starships. He hoped one day to witness a display of her power.

He joined them in the lift and saluted, trying to ignore his hair standing on end. The queen smiled again, her translucent turquoise eyes shimmering in the lift's light. A visor and respirator obscured T'vos's face while Beto stared at him with big round eyes. It unnerved him.

The lift came to a stop, and he let the members of the alliance step out first. Before him, the string of alliance members trickled into the council chambers. Despite himself, a small surge of hope radiated through his body. This feeling had nothing to with the queen, though her beauty was unparalleled, and everything to do with seeing the alliance gathering.

In a few moments, he might feel differently. As Admiral Ackon had said, the news about Lord Khelveliz wasn't something the alliance would enjoy. But seeing everyone here was reassuring—together, they could end this threat.

Just as he was about to enter the door and pass the guards, footfalls approached from behind. He turned towards the admiral and gave a quick nod. The admiral proceeded before him into the narrow corridor.

Kaytrix followed, struck once more with the sweet scent of blooms from the burning candles. He rounded the corner, passing through the archway and entering the larger corridor that led to the curved table. Bright light highlighted all the expressive colors the allies wore and the diversity of their skin, armor, and fur.

Quiet murmurs echoed throughout the large room as everyone took a seat and prepared to listen to the following discussion. He stood off to the side of the admiral and the council members while the allies filled the rest of the table.

The room was quiet for a second, and he tried to read the allies' faces. They appeared peaceful enough, with their relaxed postures, but it was obvious in their furrowed brows they suspected something. The way T'res K'netch kept glancing over to Rix Varkors suggested they'd talked about what they would discuss in this emergency meeting.

Karva Norda stood. He glanced warily at Perseph and Sarneft before beginning. "Thank you for gathering here today on such brief notice. It is with a heavy heart that I bring sad news."

The allies shared surprised glances with each other.

"Of what do you speak?" T'res bent his ears back in confusion.

Karva continued, his hands shaking as he spoke. "An enemy who call themselves the Nevo have infiltrated our protected sectors and are attacking planets. We held them at O'ber, but they eventually overpowered our forces. Since then, they have attacked Zaguarz, and we're certain the Varanus have joined forces with them."

Near silent murmurs passed between members of the alliance. Panic swept over their faces. Kaytrix studied the Shargan queen and her personal guard, T'vos. Not a single expression on the queen's face suggested she was upset. The other members didn't take the news so gracefully. Some scowled, others crossed their arms, and a few glared at Karva.

Kaytrix found it curious that Karva did not mention when this ordeal truly began, keeping their mistake and limited resources hidden, but it made sense. The damage was done, and those details weren't pertinent.

Karva took a drink of water and continued. From where Kaytrix stood, the sweat beading on Karva's forehead was prominent. He admired him for being the only council member willing to set things right. The others sat with scowls on their faces.

"It is unfortunate, but we no longer know where the Varanus' allegiance lies. The only shred of good news I have for you is that we've devised weapons that can penetrate the enemy's shields; however, our shields are still no match to their weapons fire. We've lost ships in mere seconds."

T'res cleared his throat, his yellow eyes roaming the faces of the allies sat near him. "What good is it to have these missiles if we cannot hope to face them?" He glowered at Karva. "You possess the greatest technology. If you cannot face this enemy, then we have already lost."

"I disagree," said Queen Rayla gently. "The Archarians' power is significant but has limits. If we disband now, we *will* lose. We stand a better chance if we face this enemy together."

"And what if more ships appear?" Saielis Shad demanded, crossing his arms. "The Archarians were beat by a few ships when they have fleets.

Some of us possess only a fraction of that. We cannot join in a fight to lose everything."

Nods from many of the allies followed the king's comment. They remained hesitant to subject their only forces to slaughter.

Larx Tarknic slammed a hand on the table, his entire body of armor fluid with the motion. "You will lose more than ships and the lives of your people if we do not make a stand against this enemy!" He looked at each of the members then more calmly said, "To lose people in one battle is better than to lose a kingdom."

The allies turned away from Larx, as if guilty for selfishly trying to save their ships.

Rix Varkors snorted and tossed his head from side to side. "What else do we know of this enemy?" he asked, leaning to peer at Karva.

"Not very much, I am afraid," Karva admitted, loosening the fabric around his neck. "They are terrible in close combat and their fighters lack shielding. Commander Kaytrix destroyed one vessel, but we have discovered that its counterpart is more advanced." Karva swallowed.

Kaytrix caught the councillor gazing at him with unease in his eyes.

"How do we plan to face this enemy? Can we detect their ships?" T'vos asked, his baritone voice drawing the attention of all the members.

Karva's face turned blank, and he looked to the admiral for answers.

"Commander Torex has made me aware that his crew on the *Ro'arck* are working on a way to track the Nevo's unique engine signature," Admiral Ackon said. "It's our hope to use this method to hunt their ships down." He took a breath. "We, of course, have our fleets designated to protect each of your worlds. If the enemy appears, we will be ready."

The allies nodded at this and relaxed in their seats. The talk was going better than Kaytrix had anticipated.

"If a battle is to take place," the representative of the Konsuia, Beto B'vel said, "we cannot supply enough weapons for all your needs. The missile production for the Archarians currently occupies our resources."

The allies glared at Beto, then at each other. Kaytrix could see them thinking of what Beto's statement meant. If there weren't enough weapons available, it was suicide to even try fighting.

"If we are willing to sacrifice our forces for the continuance of the alliance, we should have the weapons to do so!" snarled T'res, exposing his teeth. The fur atop his gray head bristled.

"Please," Karva Norda interrupted. "There is no need for such demands. We will uphold our promise to protect you."

"There may be another way," Queen Rayla said.

Her voice quieted the angry murmurs and disrupted the glares that flew between the allied members. She tucked a lock of turquoise-white hair behind an ear.

"And that is?" challenged T'res with a snarl, his hairs bristling again.

"Let the queen speak. She does not deserve your prodding," growled a voice from the farthest part of the round table. Chief Kovex of the Zaguarz held his head high.

A surge of guilt sank in Kaytrix's stomach for being in the chief's presence, knowing he could have fought harder to help his people.

The members settled. The chief of Zaguarz was the closest to this issue, his planet a sister to the Varanus and attacked by the enemy. The chief sat silent now. Scratches covered his face from recent tragedy. He'd escaped his planet. Now he represented a small surviving force of Zaguarz.

Queen Rayla nodded toward the chief in a silent thank you before she said, "I propose one of my soldiers assist each Archarian fleet commander. With the power we have as beings, we can turn the odds in our favor."

"No offense," Rix Varkors said with a snort, "but the Nevo can draw away the Archarians and leave our forces defenseless. If more enemy ships appear, we still face a problem with how to fight them." He crossed his arms.

"What if a Shargan were to protect each of your worlds instead?" the queen offered. "If any harm were to come, he could guard you."

Rix snorted, amused. "Again, no offense, but we know your race is but a mere handful. You cannot guarantee our planet's safety when you have fewer numbers than the rest of us."

The queen's eyes blazed with a spark of growing anger.

Chief Kovex spoke again, his voice cutting through the growing tension. "Would you like to take your chances and surrender the queen's offer? You can prove to the other systems how arrogance begets tragedy."

Rix huffed, offended, but he appeared to get Chief Kovex's message. It was a disgraceful act to mock the Shargan queen's efforts. He said no more.

"Queen Rayla, we gladly accept your generous offer," Karva said. "Our admiral will decide where we will have your soldier. Members," he addressed the allies. "It is your decision to accept the queen's offer or not. We will, however, continue with our plan for our fleets to stay protecting your worlds."

Many allied members nodded, although a few remained hesitant.

The queen looked on as a few members accepted her offer. "Very well, I will arrange it with you afterward," she said, bowing.

"Excellent." Karva said, wiping his palms on his pants. "We hope to track this enemy and not rely on your forces. I recommend you ready yourselves just to be safe. We will keep you informed on our progress. We wish you peace. Please, enjoy the beverages and food before you leave."

The allies nodded their thanks and slowly stood from the table. A few left the room immediately while others remained to talk with the other allies and the queen.

Kaytrix could feel it—the heavy burden of deceit lifting. He smiled as the representatives spoke with each other. At last, they could work together to defeat this enemy without hiding behind schemes and lies.

His gaze shifted from the primary group to focus on the Shargan queen emerging from the group. Her stunning gown was most impressive, glimmering like delicate stars. Her personal guard, T'vos, walked by her side.

"Commander Torex?" she greeted with a smile. "It is a pleasure to meet you, given the circumstances."

"Likewise." Kaytrix bowed. "I am grateful for your generous offer to the alliance. We have never fought an enemy with this kind of power."

"Yes," the queen agreed, observing him. "I have lived a long time, Commander. I have seen my fair share of war and what it does to people."

Kaytrix nodded. He'd seen it in his own people, Archarians eaten away by fighting a hopeless war, the toll it had on one's moral and physical body. "War was definitely not on my to-do list." He laughed nervously.

"Which is why I have a gift for you," Queen Rayla continued with a smile.

He took a step back, stunned. "It is unnecessary, Queen Rayla. What you've done for us today is enough."

Queen Rayla studied his hesitance. "The admiral told me you've been the sole commander charged with facing this enemy since they left O'ber," she said.

"This is true, but—"

"I sense your weariness, Commander. If you are to fight this enemy, you need energy and protection."

He studied the queen. She would never accept no for an answer. And given their unlikely situation, he could use all the help he could get.

Queen Rayla's eyes sparkled as she awaited his reply.

"That would be an honor, Queen." He bowed.

"Wonderful. I am glad you accept," She said when she offered both of her hands to him.

He grasped them, perplexed. How was she going to give him a gift this way? He gazed at her as she squeezed his hands.

"Relax, and close your eyes," she instructed.

Kaytrix obeyed when a shock traveled through his arms. He tightened his grip on her hands.

"Relax," she breathed.

He obeyed again, feeling a trickling surge travel from his fingertips through his body. It carried a cool, zapping sensation as it traveled. "Ow," he grunted, keeping his eyes closed.

"I apologize for any discomfort. It needs to adjust to the electrical current of your body," Queen Rayla answered, a hint of a smile in her voice. "You may open your eyes."

He opened his eyes and placed a hand on his tightening chest.

"Stay calm," she cautioned. "It will pass."

He swallowed, taking in another breath. The feeling was subsiding. "Thank you. I think." He grimaced.

T'vos chuckled, surprising him.

Kaytrix wanted to ask Queen Rayla a question, but Admiral Ackon burst from the crowd of allies, his face red.

"Commander!" he called as he joined them, his voice agitated. "The Konsuians report they are under attack. We must launch the *Ro'arck* regardless of its readiness. We can't allow the Nevo to take that world with all of our anti-shield weapons." His face betrayed his worry.

"Yes, Admiral! I will leave at once." Kaytrix saluted. He found himself eager to return to the battlefield and face his opponent. Mac's charred face had not left his waking eyes, and neither had his desire for justice.

He bowed to the queen and turned to walk away when she spoke.

"Wait. Take T'vos with you, to aid you on the *Ro'arck*," she urged.

T'vos looked at her. His stiff posture suggested he was not comfortable with this idea.

"No objections from either of you," she instructed. "I am returning to Sharga at once to send my soldiers."

"Very well." T'vos nodded in obedience.

Kaytrix let out a breath. "Thank you, Queen Rayla." He bowed.

Queen Rayla returned to the group of allies. He could hear her speaking in a reassuring tone about sending her soldiers. The sudden news seemed to disturb the allies. Their faces contorting into various forms of worry and anger.

Kaytrix turned toward the exit. The allies talked in hushed, worried tones. He was sure their conversations revolved around whose planet would be next.

He activated his comm. "Levro, Commander Torex here. Ready the *Ro'arck* to leave at once. We're heading to Konsuia."

As they exited the high-ceilinged room, he sensed the atmosphere change. For the first time in thousands of solar rotations, peace evaded the allies. Nothing could prepare them for the sacrifices to come.

They were going to war.

Chapter 12

Konsuia

Kaytrix entered the bridge with T'vos. He had been quiet since they left the queen's side. Was he thinking about fighting their enemy? There was no way Kaytrix could tell with his face hidden. Everything about T'vos was a mystery beneath his blue armor and faceless visor. Still, Kaytrix was glad he was here. His presence calmed his nerves.

Levro approached them, his eyes wide when he saw T'vos. "S-sir," he began, struggling to keep his gaze off T'vos. "Our primary systems are functioning as normal. The hangar is still under repair, but we've asked th e *Narvent* crew to leave for now."

Kaytrix clasped him on the shoulder. "Excellent work, Levro."

The crew arched their necks to glimpse T'vos, their eyes shining with admiration.

"Your reputation precedes you." Kaytrix glanced to T'vos. The Shargan remained standing as if made of stone, his arms casually folded behind him.

"It seems your crew has never seen one of my kind before," he said. Kaytrix detected the humor in his tone.

"That's because they haven't. Let me introduce you." He stood in the middle of the bridge and extended a hand to T'vos. "Everyone, I would like you to meet T'vos. He will aid us on the *Ro'arck* for our next mission."

T'vos bowed to the crew, acknowledging their silent admiration. In return, they saluted.

"T'vos, would you manage the shield station? You will have direct access to any system that requires energy." He turned to the crew. "The Nevo are attacking Konsuia. We are to protect the planet at all costs. Are we ready?" he asked, glancing from one station to another.

"Coordinates for Konsuia set, Commander," Nat announced from the pilot's chair.

Levro and various bridge officers nodded their readiness, a spark of vigor in their eyes.

"Let's proceed." Kaytrix sat in his command chair and drew in a breath. Nerves were humming under his skin. Khelveliz's green eyes and grating voice surfaced in his memory, poking at his confidence. What if they couldn't stop Lord Khelveliz at Konsuia? The weapons the Konsuians made were the only means of fighting the Nevo lord. What if all the alliance fell because of him? Kaytrix breathed in. *Focus.* He needed to believe they had a chance. T'vos was with them now.

Picturing his parents' faces and the mountains of home reminded him he wasn't fighting only for the alliance's unity, but for the people he loved. His role was too great a burden to carry otherwise.

The *Ro'arck* disconnected from the *Narvent,* traveling a safe distance before engaging its primary thrusters. At his command, a portal opened, and they charged through.

Their arrival to Konsuia was instant. Before them, a massive confrontation in orbit. A closer inspection of his screens revealed six Varanus ships attacking their Archarian ships, who were holding their ground. But the Varanus flexed their might, cornering the weakest vessels to destroy them first.

So far, there was nothing on his screens to determine whether Varanus ground troops were on the surface of Konsuia. If there were, the Archarians would need to send in their own troops.

"Satki, contact the Konsuians on the surface and determine what their situation is. Also, see if the Varanus will respond to any communication from us. Everyone else, I want us to focus on keeping the Varanus from attacking the planet and destroying our ships. Move us in closer and be ready to engage."

As they approached the battlefield, two Varanus cruisers launched their attack. The orange energy struck their shields fiercely.

"I am assuming they don't want to talk?" he asked, glancing over to Satki. He hated the idea of fighting the Varanus, but if this was their choice, they had to live with the consequences.

"That's right, Commander." She brushed her bangs away from her eyes. "Also, the Konsuians report there is no invasion on the surface."

Good news. It would give them a chance to secure the planet faster.

"All batteries open fire. Target the Varanus engines and disable them. Let's avoid bloodshed as much as possible."

The bridge flashed with the bombardment of orange fire, yet there was no chaos. It was a completely different experience.

T'vos stood at his station, his body an illumination of energy wisps dancing around a semi-solid center.

"How are the shields, T'vos?"

The Shargan tilted his head slightly, as if the mere sound of his voice was a distraction.

"Shields are being sustained by the enemy's attack," T'vos said, bracing himself against the console as the energy continued to flow peacefully around him.

Kaytrix couldn't decide if T'vos was in pain, or if the experience of energy flowing through his body was enjoyable. His black visor created a sense of mystery, leaving Kaytrix with questions. "How can you absorb, manipulate, convert, and redirect energy? How does that work?" he asked.

T'vos breathed in slowly. "By accessing the energy of the shields, I can reroute the attack and repurpose it to other areas. In this case, the shields."

Interesting. Kaytrix returned his attention to the battle. They had all the attention of the Varanus cruisers now, allowing the other Archarian vessels to regroup in Konsuia's orbit.

"Sir, the Varanus ships are focusing their attack on us," Levro announced, his voice stressed.

From his seat, Kaytrix could see the young man already sweating profusely. "Easy, Lieutenant. Drozah, target their power cells. Disable their ships and see if they will surrender."

Fire from the *Ro'arck* flew through the brief space between them, striking multiple targets at once. Other batteries pelted the ships in small bursts, hitting their shields. One ship ceased fire and floated powerless in space. The remaining five continued their barrage. This isn't what he had expected to happen. He had assumed they'd be through their shields by now.

"Status?" he asked.

Levro wiped his brow and swallowed. "Commander, the vessels are resisting our firepower. Our weapons don't have the same effectiveness as before."

His screen confirmed the lieutenant's report. At this rate, they could be here for a half rotation. How was this possible?

"Kersa, run a diagnostic on the ships."

"Sir, my readings indicate their ships are slightly modified." She held his gaze for a moment. "No doubt the Nevo provided them with the knowledge."

He bristled in anger, tightening his fists. If every ship turned against them gained modified shields, it would decrease their chances of success in every mission.

"Is there any way we can concentrate our fire to make our attacks more effective?"

Tuce's bright blue eyes appeared in front of him, a wide smile on his face. "Sir!" He exclaimed. "I have been monitoring T'vos's ability to strengthen our shields. It's possible he could also convert the energy to make our weapons more efficient! But . . ." his voice trailed off.

Kaytrix rose an eyebrow. "But what?"

Tuce fumbled with his portable holo-screen. "W-well, it means that he would have to redirect all his efforts from reinforcing the shields' strength."

It wasn't that bad of a sacrifice. If, for a second, they could achieve their desired goal of disabling the enemy ships, then it would be worth it. Anything was better than prolonging this fight.

"T'vos, are you able to accomplish such a task?"

There was a slight pause on the bridge as the energy around T'vos pulsed a more brilliant color of blue.

"Yes, Commander, but all the controls will go through me. Switching from one function to another will take its toll on my functionality."

It made sense T'vos would have mental limits in his ability to control the weapons and the shields. T'vos was a being of pure energy, but an entire process was happening in his body at the speed of light. They couldn't comprehend the complexity of what that process entailed.

Kaytrix took in a deep breath and exhaled. "Okay. Switch over to weapons. We'll put an end to this attack."

A slight hum came from T'vos as he made the switch. From his station, his body danced in fiery hues of blue and white, his body a mere mirage.

Kaytrix noticed the Shargan's actions distracted the crew as they peered up from their holo-screens, mouths agape.

"Attention on your stations," Kaytrix reminded them gruffly. Their heads snapped back to their consoles but even he found himself compelled to glance at T'vos performing the miracles of his race.

Several large blasts of energy ripped from the *Ro'arck's* guns. The attack hit the closest Varanus vessel, incapacitating it immediately.

"Wooo!" the crew cheered.

The other Varanus vessels moved off to avoid the same fate. As they fled, the *Ro'arck* turned to pursue them, disabling the vessel in seconds. Kaytrix couldn't believe T'vos's capabilities. He only wished their partnership could have happened earlier to spare the lives of his squad, Mac, and so many other Archarians.

"Sir!" Kersa shrieked.

Her voice shattered his concentration. He turned from the fight to see her pale white face. "Lord Khelveliz's ship just dropped out of a hyperspace jump."

Dread stopped his heartbeat. "T'vos, switch to shields!"

The order came too late. The *Ro'arck* swayed from a massive attack as the green energy slipped through their shields. It crawled along their hull like some possessed ghost, damaging everything it touched.

Red and yellow lights flashed on the bridge, casting their woeful colors on the surrounding crew. Sirens called out in warning for various systems, and alerts scrolled across his screen. The hit was critical.

"Sir, we've sustained hull damage and lost control of various forward section turrets," Levro reported.

"I have shields again," T'vos announced, his voice strained from the effort.

T'vos had warned them. If this were to happen again, Kaytrix would have to be careful in his tactics fighting Lord Khelveliz.

"Status report!"

"Sir, two Varanus vessels remain fully operational," Levro rattled off. "Our sister ships remain in formation."

This could go one of two ways, and he couldn't let his fear of losing Konsuia or their other ships outweigh the chance they had of destroying Lord Khelveliz.

"Target Lord Khelveliz's ship with the new missiles. Don't give him a chance to get away or destroy our ships. The rest of the fleet can manage the last of the Varanus vessels."

"Yes, sir," Levro acknowledged.

The *Ro'arck* turned to pursue Lord Khelveliz's ship, firing several new missiles at them. They hit their target, piercing through the shield and causing damage. The ship returned fire, but the energy hit the shields, funneled through T'vos, and rerouted back into keeping the shields strong.

The black ship sped out of targeting range and ceased fire, as if the effectiveness of the *Ro'arck's* shields shocked them. Pride filled Kaytrix's chest, but he tried not to forget the enemy they were fighting. The last encounter had almost ended in their destruction.

"Sir, Lord Khelveliz is hailing us," Satki said. "Should I accept?"

Kaytrix took a quick breath in and out to prepare himself. He wasn't fond of the last impression Lord Khelveliz had left on him. He wanted nothing more than to shoot him out of the sky, but a part of him cautioned not to be hasty.

"What's the status of our sister ships?"

"They are holding the line," Levro reported.

"Very well. Answer the call, Satki, but let's be prepared to get in range and attack if he makes a move to escape."

"Yes, sir," the crew acknowledged.

A sudden flash of holographic light pierced the yellow and red flashing on their bridge. For a moment, the wails were silenced, the connection of the communication taking precedence in the systems. In the display, Lord Khelveliz appeared standing. Impressed? Aggravated? It was hard to determine, but his eyes burned with the same evil glow as before.

"Commander Torex," he said in his sibilant voice.

"Lord Khelveliz," Kaytrix acknowledged. He half expected the same darkness to leach through the display and latch onto him, but after a moment, Lord Khelveliz locked his mechanical arms across his chest.

"I see you've made some impressive advancements since our last encounter," Lord Khelveliz hissed. His eyes roamed Kaytrix's background as if searching for something.

Kaytrix viewed his holographic projection of what Khelveliz could see. Thankfully, T'vos was not in view.

"I see you have also made advancements of your own. Interesting promise you made to the Varanus. I'd like to warn you, though, that their appetite for glory is enormous. Careful how quickly you advance their ships."

A terrifying screech escaped Khelveliz. "You think you've got an edge on me, *Torex*, but let me remind you, I have the upper hand in this fight. I will soon discover your alternative power source and its secrets. I only need to get my hands on one of you . . ."

Kaytrix flinched, remembering the crushing feeling of fingers around his throat. So, their *alternative power source* troubled Lord Khelveliz? Is that the only reason he stopped attacking?

"I'd like to see you try, honestly." Kaytrix was enjoying his moment of success. So many Archarians had died bringing them to this moment. To have the enemy apprehensive of their ability was a glorious feeling.

Lord Khelveliz flashed his eyes and green light glowed on his face, marking certain parts of his armor.

"You think you're better than me?" he asked.

Kaytrix hesitated. Did he think that? "I don't murder innocent people for personal gain, so yeah."

Lord Khelveliz's body recoiled backwards at his words. An angered roar erupted from his body like a bursting volcano. He slashed his consoles with his daggered fingers. Sparks flew across the dark space, and he pressed his face to the display, taking up the entire image of the hologram.

"Your race are the true *murderers*, Commander Torex. Do not lecture me on killing innocent lives." He hissed, stepping back to throw his cloak over his shoulder. "And I have news for you and your *pathetic* council. With your limited reach, your allies are surrendering to *me* as we speak. When they have all turned against you, your entire planet will burn!"

Lord Khelveliz's dark voice wrung Kaytrix's heart dry of any feeling of success he possessed. The communication ended and he snapped to.

"Target his ship!" he called out.

But the black vessel had already turned and gone, taking with it the last two Varanus ships.

They protected Konsuia successfully, but what Lord Khelveliz said disturbed him. If worlds were under attack, the allies should have called for help. Khelveliz had to be lying. But as he tried to disregard the Nevo's words, doubt crept into his mind.

What if Lord Khelveliz was telling the truth?

Chapter 13

ENEMIES

Lord Khelveliz's claims were bold, unbelievable even, but Kaytrix couldn't ignore his words. He needed to report back to the admiral to discover if there was truth to what the Nevo said.

There was more that disturbed him, like the mention of his race being murderers. Was Lord Khelveliz referring to O'ber and the soldiers he lost there, or the Nevo ship Kaytrix destroyed? As much as he loathed Lord Khelveliz, trying to understand the root of his anger was becoming a pastime. How could someone want to destroy an entire race for no reason? Or was there a reason?

The *Ro'arck* approached Archaria and the *Narvent* station as he finished his musings. The bridge crew were silent as they carried on their duties. The wails of the damaged systems temporarily deactivated, allowing him to think clearer about what he was about to say to Admiral Ackon.

"Satki, hail Admiral Ackon from here. I need to speak to him immediately," he said, annoyed.

He filled in the admiral on their mission, but he wasn't prepared for the admiral's response.

"Admiral, what Lord Khelveliz is saying cannot be true!" Kaytrix stood, infuriated. "We just met with the alliance members. Everything was fine."

"It appears that while they attended our meeting, he orchestrated several attacks," Admiral Ackon's voice crackled through the comm. "After you left, we received multiple reports of Varanus infiltration, both aerial and with ground forces. Their strategy is to take control of a planet's arkross and then the planet."

"Enabling them to prevent the inhabitants from escaping and acquiring help." Kaytrix gritted his teeth. Lord Khelveliz was telling the truth. "I don't understand this *Nevo's* hatred for us. What did we do to provoke his anger?" In that moment he wished Mac had decoded the files, especially missions 3199 and 3200—the same missions Perseph mentioned, the missions that started all of this.

There was an uncomfortable pause and he waited for Ackon to reply. "Did we lose him?" he asked Satki.

"No, sir. Connection is ongoing," she said.

"Still here. My apologies, Commander Torex. There's a lot happening here and with the allies. We have launched the fleets to their designated posts. Those who have accepted the Shargans' protection are first in line. We will worry about other worlds outside the alliance later. It sounds like T'vos was a major factor in your victory today. Perhaps the queen would consider offering more soldiers to aid our ships?"

Kaytrix glanced to T'vos. He stood supporting himself against the console, his body quivering in the dim light of the bridge. The battle had exhausted him. They would need more than the Shargans' help to win this war.

"Yes, sir, but this isn't a solution. T'vos can help, but he has his limitations. As for the other planets, is it wise to allow them to fall? There must be something we can do to stop the Varanus."

"Our closest allies are our priority if we are to survive," retorted Ackon. "But you are right. There is something we can do about the Varanus: destroy their arkross. Without the ability to walk troops onto worlds, they will have to resort to transporting soldiers. It won't stop them for long, but it's the start."

"Affirmative, sir," Kaytrix said.

"Report back when you have completed your mission."

The communication ended.

Kaytrix grunted and held his chin. He was not looking forward to facing the ferocious tribes of the Varanus. Lord Khelveliz was wise to use them as his army; the alliance was in for a challenge.

"Set coordinates for Varanus?" Nat asked.

"Yes, and prepare to face an armada of Varanus starships," Kaytrix cautioned. Facing Lord Khelveliz was one thing, but facing an ally was another.

The *Ro'arck* arrived at Varanus instantly. Alarms sounded in warning as multiple signals appeared on the scanners. Red lights flooded the bridge deck, setting everyone on edge. Before them, a fleet of Varanus ships prowled the space around the planet.

"We are being hailed," Satki announced. "It's from one of the lead ships."

"Let's see it," Kaytrix acknowledged. Would it be the same ship from their last encounter, the rebel leader who bought into Lord Khelveliz's promises of greater glory?

A Varanus appeared in a blue silhouette of light. His vicious snarl exposed a set of sharp canines, best suited for ripping flesh. The tendrils atop his scaled head locked in anger.

"You are trespassing, Archarian. Leave at once, or we will destroy your ship!" the Varanus demanded in a fierce growl.

Something was different about the Varanus's reptilian eyes. A green haze smoked in the once vibrant pupils. It looked familiar . . .

"Your world has broken our alliance and abused the gift of the arkross. I can no longer respect your wishes. I am here to prevent you from further atrocities. Stand aside, or face warfare," Kaytrix said.

"This is our space. Trespass, and you will die!"

"I am afraid I have to," he countered.

The Varanus threw his head back and roared. "Then you will die today, Archarian!" he breathed, pointing a scaly finger at him.

Their communication ended. As much as the Varanus were their enemy in this moment, Kaytrix couldn't let that turn his heart cold to them. There was more going on here than Varanus seizing an opportunity for glory. An ulterior power was at play and he suspected it had something to do with Lord Khelveliz.

"Head for the planet. We will avoid fighting if we can. If their shields are modified, we will get stuck fighting an endless battle. Let's get in and out," he said.

Kaytrix observed the crew members at their stations. They braced themselves as Nat gripped the controls and approached the fleet.

The Varanus ships attacked. Compared to the Archarians, their weapons possessed less strength, but their tactics were proving astoundingly aggressive.

"They are targeting our life support systems," Levro reported.

Yes, more aggressive than usual, Kaytrix thought. "Shield status?"

"The shields are holding steady thanks to T'vos, sir," reported Lieutenant Levro.

"Excellent." He nodded, pleased. He observed how Nat handled the *Ro'arck* through the sea of ships, impressed at how she drifted the *Ro'arck* up and over ships without the slightest hesitation. She controlled the ship as if she were born in the pilot's chair.

"Searching for the arkross now, Commander," Kersa announced. "It is near the lower continent. I am sending coordinates to you, Nat."

"Coordinates received. Proceeding with your permission, Commander?" Nat requested, narrowly missing a collision with a Varanus starship.

"Permission granted. Let's destroy it and get out of here," he said, wincing at Nat's narrow escape from the other ship.

They were nearing the end of the Varanus fleet. The blockade of ships had made it impossible to access the planet, but Nat maneuvered the *Ro'arck* in a way it hadn't flown before.

She pushed the throttle forward, giving the *Ro'arck* the speed it needed to exit the blockade and head toward the planet. Through the viewport, the opening toward their exit was growing larger when a ship arrived out of hyperspace. A knot of anxiety tightened in his stomach.

"Sir, it's Lord Khelveliz," Levro announced.

Kaytrix hesitated, the grating words of the Nevo returning to scratch at his confidence.

"Sir?" Levro probed.

Kaytrix snapped out of his daze, ignoring the knot in his stomach and the doubt in his mind. He could not allow fear to influence his decisions.

"Proceed with the plan. The Varanus must cease advancements on other worlds."

The *Ro'arck* continued its course for the planet. Kaytrix observed the black ship, poised before them, solid as a mountain. The massive vessel showed no signs of wavering, and he started questioning his decision. The *Ro'arck's* proximity to the ship was becoming dangerous.

"Nat!" he called.

"Trust me," she growled.

He tried to anchor himself to his chair, allowing Nat to follow through with her decision. They were drawing closer to the vessel when, in the last second, Nat guided the *Ro'arck* into a nosedive, avoiding a collision with the Nevo ship and passing beneath its underbelly.

Shrieks of surprise left the officers and Nat engaged the full throttle again, sending them straight for the planet. They passed through the blockade successfully.

"Sorry, Commander!" she yelled.

"Just keep us in one piece," he grumbled. Even though the *Ro'arck* had great inertia dampeners, quick movements like that with the antigravity made him nauseous.

They entered the atmosphere of Varanus, their shields blazing red upon re-entry.

"Approaching target, Drozah," Nat said.

"Make the first shot count. We don't have the luxury to muck around," Drozah cautioned Zenro beside him as they prepared to destroy the arkross.

"I have it targeted," Zenro announced. "Sir, I can't take the shot."

"Why not?" demanded Drozah, shoving the smaller man out of the way.

Kaytrix understood Zenro. The officer must have seen the Varanus soldiers surrounding the arkross in the thousands. It was natural to shy away from the order of killing thousands.

He shuddered. Standing toe to toe against an army of angry Varanus soldiers was no desire of his. Their chances of surviving that kind of warfare were zero, even with their advancements. And he couldn't allow the allies to face that kind of battle either. The admiral was right in sending them on this mission.

"Coming around for another shot. We can't mess this up," Nat announced, a hint of annoyance in her voice.

The *Ro'arck* received a blast, shaking the ship.

"Status?" Kaytrix asked. He glanced to T'vos. The Shargan was clearly growing tired from handling all the energy, his body trembling.

"Lord Khelveliz is trying to weaken our shields with concentrated fire!" reported Lieutenant Levro.

He might just prevail, Kaytrix thought. He focused back on Drozah. "Forget about targeting the arkross," he said. He hated to give his next order, but it had to be done. "Drop bombs if you have to."

He received a blank stare from Zenro, but Drozah got to work and initiated the bomb drop sequence. Kaytrix hoped Zenro wouldn't think less of him for the decision. This was war.

Focused energy roared from the turrets, colliding with the arkross frame. Following behind was a sequence of bombs, dropping and exploding on impact. The portal device weakened, forcing the frame to buckle and the energy within its core to erupt. The arkross burst into pieces, releasing its energy in a wave of destruction through the thousands of soldiers and the surrounding city.

Kaytrix's heart pained. It was a victory for them, but a tremendous loss for the Varanus. This event could affect their future relations.

"Return to Archaria," he ordered. He was aware that T'vos was reaching his limit in handling the strain of energy flowing through his body.

The *Ro'arck* breached orbit and another obstacle awaited them: the blockade of Varanus ships. Ominously they waited, poised, ready to strike; their patience had brought them this moment.

Their fleet unleashed a destructive barrage of weapons fire upon the *Ro'arck* with great intensity. The *Ro'arck's* forward shields blazed red in resistance. As the menacing colors possessed the crew's faces, Kaytrix could see their panic.

"Sir, we can't open a hyperspace portal with that many ships in our flight path. I need an opening now or we're done for!" Nat said.

They were heading toward the awaiting armada. If they couldn't leave, T'vos would fail in holding the shields and the enemy would destroy the *Ro'arck*.

"Drozah, see what you can do," Kaytrix said.

Drozah fired their weapons, but there were too many ships. Lord Khelveliz attacked them from behind, sending the *Ro'arck's* systems into a fit of flashing red lights and wails.

"Ugh!" Nat fumed, dodging another wave of weapons fire.

They needed to get past the barricade. Only a bit farther until they could engage the portal.

A singular blast rocked the ship. Sirens wailed louder. Warnings flashed at Kaytrix. Half the command bridge's controls turned red and ceased to function.

"I have lost power to several sub-light engines, Commander," Nat announced in a panic. "I don't know what happened."

On his screens, nothing indicated they'd lost shields yet. T'vos groaned. He turned to see the Shargan gripping his console.

"My apologies," T'vos struggled to say as his fingers melted the panels. "I'm using all the energy to clear us a path."

Kaytrix clenched his jaw. A cleared path ensured a successful portal opening, but it didn't come without risks. What T'vos proposed was risky. Could they make it through the portal in one piece?

"Don't hesitate, T'vos! It's now or never," Kaytrix said.

A column of pure energy emitted from the *Ro'arck's* main cannon. The intense focus of the attack carved a hole through any Varanus ship blocking them. The aggressiveness of the energy stunned Kaytrix; it had the diameter of a small moon. Just as suddenly as it appeared, the energy faded, leaving in its wake a clear-cut route.

Wails of the *Ro'arck's* sirens increased in urgency, red lights drowning the bridge. He glanced at T'vos's station but did not see him.

"Get us home!" he roared.

The portal opened and enemy weapons fire flew towards them in a frenzy. The *Ro'arck* struggled through the path carved out for her, shuddering in rebellion of what Nat asked of her.

His heart slowed; the portal gleamed before them. It was so close. Green energy from the enemy raced past them. They sailed through the wreckage left by T'vos.

Closer now.

The *Ro'arck* groaned. The crew gasped as they passed through the threshold of the portal and arrived on the other side in one piece. He almost couldn't believe it. Peacefully before them rotated their beloved home world and the *Narvent* station.

"Satki," he said. "Ask the *Narvent* to dispatch medical crews. Have them standing by when we dock."

"Copy that, Commander," Satki said.

Kaytrix shook his head, still processing their near-death experience. "Levro, can you explain to me what happened?"

"One second, sir," Levro replied, sifting through information as he spoke with Tuce. He looked back up at Kaytrix while referencing to his data. "T'vos used our lower cannon to focus the energy he harnessed to carve us a path. He destroyed it in the process while protecting the ship."

He nodded as the ship's medics arrived on the bridge. He hoped T'vos's efforts had not cost him his life. This was a troubled time to lose such an important part of their crew.

He resumed oversight of the docking sequence and checked the systems, noting that the engine they lost was completely cut off from the power source, making it safe to dock. The replacement of an entire engine and a turret could be a problem. Longer repairs took time from him he didn't have to spare.

The *Ro'arck* aligned with the *Narvent* and docked. Waiting medical personnel rushed through the port to the ship and arrived on the bridge in moments. Kaytrix wanted to help with T'vos, but he needed to obtain the *Ro'arck's* damage report for the engineers first.

"We're going to need that crystal for the engineers," he said to Levro.

"Yes, sir. I am on it," Levro replied.

He was proud of Levro in that moment for his insight. He glanced behind him as the medics assisted T'vos and then he looked back at his screen, trying to distract himself from his sudden emotions. The monitors told a sad story for the *Ro'arck.*

Nat rose from her seat and approached the medics. "Will he be alright?" she asked.

One medic stood by with a holo-chart, inputting information as his companions readied T'vos for transport.

"It's hard for me to say. His biology differs completely from ours."

The medical officer joined the others and hurried T'vos onto a hover-stretcher. In moments, they were moving him to the medical center.

Kaytrix closed his eyes, knowing this couldn't be good. With a severely damaged ship and T'vos injured, standing against Lord Khelveliz was impossible. He tried to hide his worry from Nat.

She gazed into his eyes. "What do we do now?" she asked, tucking her thumbs into the pockets of her pants.

He drew in a breath. "We keep fighting. In any way we can." It was easier said than done— anything in life was. But when it came down to it, could he face Lord Khelveliz and fight as bravely as they had before?

He turned to address his crew. "May I have your attention, please. We accomplished our mission today, but with that victory we experienced a setback. The *Ro'arck* is incapacitated. Until the repairs are completed, I request you gather your strength and provide your skills where you can. The sooner we can get back into the fight, the better. You are dismissed."

The crew drug their feet as they left their stations. They weren't alone in their exhaustion. Was having a Shargan aboard still exciting for them? He allowed himself a small smile. Without T'vos, the mission could have ended differently.

Lieutenant Levro approached, handing him the crystal.

"Thank you, Lieutenant. I want you to oversee the engineers and keep me informed on the progress of the repairs."

"Yes, sir." Levro saluted.

"And Levro," he said, watching as the lieutenant's thin form halted.

"Yes, sir?"

"Good job out there."

Levro nodded, a glimmer of appreciation in his eyes, before turning to resume his duties.

The engineers gathered on the bridge and ran their diagnostics. They moved among the exiting crew, muttering with each other. One approached him, seeking the crystal. He handed it to him, and the engineer inserted it into the reader. The man read for a few moments and cussed under his breath, shooting a judgmental look at Kaytrix.

"I am convinced they tire of seeing the *Ro'arck* come through," Kaytrix said to Nat once the man had walked away.

Nat nodded. "I bet they won't complain once they hear what we did today."

He wasn't so sure. He wished he could return at least once without the *Ro'arck* falling to pieces. With the severe state of the *Ro'arck* and T'vos, they couldn't go anywhere. That alone could have disastrous repercussions, especially with an angry Nevo lord on the hunt for their blood.

Kaytrix turned from Nat to begin standard protocol and his least favorite thing: reporting to command.

Chapter 14

BAD NEWS

Kaytrix left the command center scratching his head. Relaying their mission's success to the admiral hadn't gone as he'd expected. Instead of praise, the admiral directed him to meet with the councillors immediately. Why wouldn't the admiral tell him what was going on?

As he approached the lift, the grating voice of Lord Khelveliz echoed in his mind: *With your limited reach, your allies are surrendering to me as we speak.*

The words jarred him. Were they a prelude to what transpired in the brief time he was away? He passed through the doors of the council chamber and entered the dimly lit space. The air was thick. The sweet incense wasn't burning, highlighting the stale smell of body heat.

Kaytrix entered the inner chambers. The Shrovon leader, the King of Cordabo, Saielis Shad, and Kovex gathered around the crescent table, scowling at the council in silence. Where were the other allies?

Queen Rayla stood separate from the gathering, observing them from a distance. She appeared deep in thought, but her posture hinted at more. She held her head in one hand, the other supporting her elbow. Whatever was on her mind burdened her. She acknowledged his presence and lowered her hands.

He entered the round room, and the allies turned their attention to him, their faces fit with rage and disappointment. As he neared the crescent table, Queen Rayla gracefully approached him.

"What's going on?" he whispered. He had never seen the allies so angry.

"Kaytrix, I am glad you made it back. The meeting is just ending," the queen uttered, her tone soft, barely audible. "It's gotten worse since the last gathering."

He studied her face, then glanced to the gathering of their allies. "Meaning?"

Queen Rayla hesitated, contemplating her words.

He waited.

"Many worlds outside the alliance have succumbed to Lord Khelveliz's brutal power. Several allies have submitted to him, pledging to follow him to spare their cities," she said.

He shook his head, sinking into disbelief. "How did this happen? I thought our new missiles and the Shargans were enough to hold off their ships?"

"That's just it. Lord Khelveliz attacks everyone at once. Our forces get held up and spread thin. The remaining allies are demanding more protection. They are threatening to leave the alliance if Archaria ignores their requests. A few have already parted ways." She pointed to the group before them. "These few continue with us, but it is hard on them."

He grimaced at the overload of information. It was as though they were fighting two wars—one political and one on the front lines.

"What of your soldiers? Have they left the allies who have turned?" he asked, his tone softening.

She sighed and lowered her gaze. "Some made it back to our planet. The others have not contacted me."

He remembered T'vos then, and the sacrifice he had made to ensure their safe return to Archaria. Were all Shargan soldiers so selfless?

"Don't worry about T'vos," she said. "He will slowly recover. If it happens again, he will return to our planet."

He gazed at the queen. Was his worry for T'vos obvious? "Lord Khelveliz was right," he said, his mood bleak. "Our allies are fracturing, and we can't protect them."

It was as though he was living a nightmare. Archaria and the alliance had been strong for thousands of solar rotations. With a few well-aimed strikes, they were on their knees, some even begging for mercy.

He searched the wise queen's eyes, wishing she could restore his hope in his people and their abilities. He yearned for words that could comfort the unrest in his soul.

Queen Rayla peered at her hands, appearing to struggle with the alliance's deterioration.

He returned his gaze to the meeting where Karva Norda rose, uttering words of a sad farewell. The allied members dispersed. While leaving, they cast worried glances his way. They knew Archaria had failed them, and he did too. It crushed him. Everything he was fighting to protect was being destroyed.

Karva approached them while Perseph and Sarneft slithered out of the room. It was clear they held little interest in speaking with him. He scoffed. No loss there.

"Were you able to satisfy them?" he asked, redirecting his focus as the aging man drew close.

Karva appeared ill, his face pale and drenched with sweat. "We are on the brink of losing the remaining allies," he stated. "We don't have the ships for everyone."

Kaytrix crossed his arms. "If allies have left the alliance, withdraw our forces from their worlds and assign them to those who fight with us," he said. They couldn't afford to lose their remaining allies.

Karva took in a breath as if considering his suggestion. "The admiral is worried about losing ground. If we withdraw from those planets, we risk solidifying their choice to leave the alliance."

Kaytrix's jaw dropped slightly. It wasn't a good strategy. "We can't stay where we are not welcome. There is no guarantee they won't attack our ships. We are tricking ourselves into thinking we can keep our forces there."

Karva frowned. "What choice do we have? It feels like no matter what we decide, there's only one fate for us."

"Explain." He refused to believe what the councillor said. They still had a chance. Didn't they?

"The council wants to discuss an alternative plan for winning the war." Karva swallowed. "If Lord Khelveliz intends to wipe us out, as you stated, then we need to preserve our race."

Kaytrix studied Queen Rayla, hoping he imagined what the councillor said. "The council suggests we run and hide while the remaining galaxy suffers?" His lip curled as he unraveled his arms.

"They *suggest* we find an alpha site," Karva corrected. "Relocating ensures our survival. It's only a matter of time before Lord Khelveliz demands the coordinates of our world from a fallen ally."

Kaytrix fought back anger. "And what of our alliance and other innocent planets? Do we condemn them to suffer at the hands of Lord Khelveliz?"

Karva's eyes lowered as he pondered the question. "Unfortunately, we cannot help them. We've sealed our fate."

Kaytrix searched the councillor's face for any hint of deception, but there was not a wrinkle out of place. After everything they had been through with the alliance, this was how it was to end? Being an Archarian suddenly meant nothing. He hated to admit the truth, but facts were facts. With all the solar rotations of good they brought to the galaxy, it now crumbled away with a few selfish decisions.

It wasn't right to let their allies fall to Lord Khelveliz while they ran away, but Karva was right. With four allies left, Khelveliz had them beat and there was no changing the council's mind. He breathed in deep and let the morally cutting situation go for now.

"We don't have enough ships. How do we intend to evacuate everyone?" he asked, aware of his parents.

"I don't have answers for you, Commander." Karva paused. "It is time I rest. We will discuss this in the morning."

Karva dismissed himself, leaving Kaytrix standing with the queen. The room was eerie in its silence.

"I am sorry it has come to this," she breathed, touching his arm.

He shook his head. "I should be the one apologizing. I thought we could beat Lord Khelveliz. And . . ." He paused. "I really hate how the council is abandoning everyone. If the alliance knew about this, they'd help Lord Khelveliz finish us off."

Queen Rayla's eyes hardened. "You forget what has gotten you this far, Commander. It hasn't been better weapons or my help." She pointed to his heart. "It's what you love that has gotten you this far. Don't lose sight of that, or Lord Khelveliz will win."

The queen left his presence. After watching her leave, he stared out the window at the blizzard encapsulating the mountain range. In the silence of the icy walls that stood for millennia, he sensed a descending darkness of change.

Chapter 15

HOME

Kaytrix stood outside in the frigid air of Avsilan, waiting at the transit system among the civilians going about their evening. He tried to find peace among those unaware of what transpired around them, but every time he tried to feel that peace, the truth came back to cut him.

If the council was serious about moving the people to an alpha site, the likelihood of his parents making it was slim. He needed to see them one last time. He fought the hopelessness rising in his throat and trying to choke him as he boarded the transport.

Kaytrix allowed himself to forget about the *Ro'arck* as the city disappeared, replaced by the countryside. He distinctly remembered the last time he traveled out this way. It was to see his ma right after her diagnosis.

She learned ten solar rotations ago cancer was growing in her body. The treatments prevented it from spreading but could not vanquish it completely. He wished he'd studied medicine instead, but he knew himself too well. He lacked the patience to stare at things on a microscopic level.

The transport beneath him slowed, its engines whirring down until it came to a complete stop. Kaytrix rose from his seat and exited, leaving the sticky warmth of the transport to embrace the much cooler air of the mountains. His breath left his body like a ghost. He was one step closer to home after ten solar rotations.

A man greeted him from the nearest building, a tiny, dilapidated shack that lacked the advancement city buildings had. As the man approached, he spoke, but the departing transit system drowned out his voice.

"Awful sorry, sir. I couldn't hear you," Kaytrix apologized. "Could you repeat?"

"I said," began the stout fellow, "are you lost?"

Kaytrix forgot he was wearing his armor. To see a soldier this far from the city was rare.

"Thank you, but no. I am Torex's son, Kaytrix. I've come back to see him and Ma." Kaytrix forced a smile. He recognized this farmer as an old neighbor.

"Oh, Kaytrix. I remember you! Sorry, son. Err. Sir, I mean. It's me, Merl."

Kaytrix waved a hand as the windchill bit his bare neck, his ears, and the tip of his nose. He had forgotten about the embrace of the mountain cold.

"Hey, Merl, you are looking well. Don't worry about formalities. I would like to borrow a drorse," he said urgently, his teeth chattering. The man's warm words wanted to lift his spirits, but the truth cut this otherwise pleasant moment into ribbons.

Merl grinned. "You're supposed to be used to the cold, being up in space and all," he teased, leading Kaytrix to the nearby barn. "You can pick any you fancy. I am sure it would honor any of them to sport you," Merl teased again. "Need help with their gear?"

Kaytrix entered the building. The familiar scents of animals, dried grass, and sweet feed greeted him at the door. He'd almost forgotten them.

"Well, 'A true Archarian farmer never forgets the roots from which he sprang. For it is always in his heart and in the folds of his hands,'" Kaytrix quoted.

"Very good!" Merl beamed. "A quote from the *Farmer's Beginning*. I am impressed. I'll get you some tack."

Kaytrix nodded, choking on his emotions as he went to thank Merl. He turned to face the array of stalls before him.

Eyes of drorse peered back at him, content in their warmth. One greeted him with a soft nicker, placing her head over the stall and sniffing him. Large, pointed ears on her head rotated forward.

"Hello," he said. He stroked the thick fur of the animal.

The drorse tossed her head up and down, nickering more.

"Don't be afraid. Do you want a treat?" He reached into a sack hanging off the nearby door and grabbed a few dried fruits.

The mare drorse nibbled them delightedly out of his hand. He admired her thick roan mane and crisp blue eyes

"Well, well, she knows a farm boy when she sees one," Merl said. "Here's her tack."

Kaytrix grimaced as he led the tall animal out of the stall and secured a rope around her neck. Next was the blanket and thin hide saddle. The practice soothed him.

While Merl drew the barn doors apart, Kaytrix reflected on Queen Rayla's words. He scolded himself. He had to believe they had a chance at fighting Lord Khelveliz.

Kaytrix mounted the saddled drorse and nodded his thanks to Merl. He guided the animal beneath him with the pressure of his legs and the slight touch of the reins on her neck. They started at a walk and then a slow canter. Kaytrix found his rhythm with the drorse, and soon they traveled together as one.

The snow and wind bit at Kaytrix's face, but he couldn't care less. Being home in the mountains after many rotations was a gift. One he should have given himself a long time ago. It was comforting to see the mountains and trees, all topped with a fresh layer of snow. To hear the soft *plot-plot, plot-plot* of the drorse beneath him, to feel the warmth of her on his legs, to smell the sweetness of her breath, and to feel the warmth of her exhales . . .

Kaytrix was more alive inside than he had been for a long time. Even to see the little fields, all covered in their blankets of snow, made his heart glad. He could not wait to see his ma and father again.

The drorse slowed at his command and snorted; she had run a long distance for him. They followed a winding road past several other farmhouses, neighbors of his family since he was little. Then finally the road reached its end, leading to a tiny house crowded out by the trees planted as a perimeter many rotations ago. A warm light flickered in the main window as silhouettes passed in front.

Kaytrix rode through the entrance of the property—a huge, open gate—then to the barn, where he dismounted the drorse. He threw down some dried feed and put water in a bucket.

"Thanks, girl," he said lovingly with a pat to her side of thick fur.

He slid out into the cold once more, wrapping his cloak around himself and tossing his hood over his head. The walk to the house was short, but the wicked wind flying over the mountains and through the fields chased him down and made the last leg of his journey more difficult.

Finally, he reached the door. Just as he was about to knock, it cracked open slightly and a pair of familiar eyes peered out at him from behind its safety.

Warmth from the house embraced his face, and the smell of a freshly baked cake warmed his heart with memories.

"Kaytrix?" his father uttered, a look of disbelief on his face. "Quick, come inside before the cold gobbles you up." He chuckled, opening the door wider and ushering him in.

"Who is it?" called a voice from the other room. The cheerful sound of his mother's voice softened his heart.

His dad took his cloak and hung it up to defrost. "Ahna, you won't believe who it is!" he exclaimed, rushing into the next room.

"Well, don't leave me in suspense, Kent, tell me who is here to visit?" Kaytrix could hear his ma chatting away. "If it is the neighbor for some more supplies, we haven't any. You know that, right? What's left is for us, and he can . . ." Her voice trailed off as Kaytrix entered the room.

Tears welled in her eyes. "Oh, my dear boy! You've come home!" She beamed, reaching up for a hug.

"Yes, Ma, I am home. I am sorry it's been too long." Kaytrix held her thin form.

"Oh, shhh. That does not matter now." Memories of being a boy flashed before his eyes as her comfort washed through him. He took a step back, and she sat in her rocker. It had undoubtedly become her preferred place to sit as her energy dissipated from treatments.

"Let us have something warm to celebrate your visit." She gazed around to room as if looking for his father. She hid her mouth with an open hand to the side. "Your father has become quite the cook lately. Under my supervision, of course," she whispered.

Kaytrix laughed with her and glanced to his father, who entered the room. A rim of tears lined his eyes. Kaytrix could only assume seeing her laughing and smiling brought him much relief. He blinked them away and entered the kitchen. In a few moments, he returned with the cake he baked with serving utensils and dishes.

Kaytrix made himself comfortable on the furniture next to his mom. The aroma of the freshly baked cake and displayed images of his family flooded him with memories. It was the same warm space he remembered from when he was a boy. Absolutely nothing had changed, for which he was glad.

"How did you get here?" asked his ma, grasping his hand and holding it in hers. Her hand was small and frail. Another reminder of the importance of seeing them in person.

"I borrowed a drorse. She's in the barn for now," Kaytrix said. "How are you feeling?"

Ma's face fell, and she shook her head. "I have my days. The medication has helped. Thank you," she said simply, patting his hand. "I am so glad you are here." She smiled again, blinking away more tears.

Kaytrix wiped them from her face with a finger. "Me too," he said, glancing back to his dad.

"How long are you able to stay, son? A couple of days?" his dad inquired, passing out cake before settling into an old chair opposite them. He took a bite, waiting for an answer.

Kaytrix fiddled with his fork, his dad's eyes still on him expectantly. "I am not sure. This was a last-minute decision. I could be called back any time."

"How goes your new post you told us about? Commanding a starship is what you have always dreamed about," his dad said, taking another bite of his cake.

Kaytrix paused. It was so long ago. What should he say to his parents? Life was stressful enough for them with his ma's health. He hesitated to add to the stress, but he also hated how the council had lied to him. He wasn't about to do the same to his parents.

"It's been an adventure." He feigned a smile and gave his dad a look as ma ate her cake, oblivious to the exchange between them. "I have the *Ro'arck* docked at the *Narvent,* undergoing slight repairs. Nothing major."

"Oh?" Kent asked as he finished the last bite of his cake. His eyes focused on his son as realization came over his face. "I see . . ."

Kaytrix said lightly, "Just some calibrations, that's all."

His father nodded. He would want to discuss what was happening.

Ma seemed oblivious to their quick exchange of looks as she nibbled at her cake. She sighed and placed the fork down.

"Tired, Ahna?" Kent asked, redirecting his focus and taking her plate.

She nodded. "I don't want to fall asleep while you are here." She yawned, gazing at him tiredly.

"It's okay, Ma, you need your rest." Kaytrix stood to kiss her forehead. "I loved being able to see you again, Ma. You take care of yourself and listen to the doctor."

Ahna smiled. "Oh, yes. Don't you worry about it, Kaytrix. I am sure that you face bigger worries than making sure your ma listens to the doctor."

Kaytrix watched fondly as his ma fell into a content sleep.

Kent rose and grabbed their dishes. "Let's chat in the kitchen," he whispered.

Kaytrix tucked his ma in with a blanket and kissed her forehead one last time. He entered the kitchen as his father drew water and started washing the plates. A simple chore that made it so much harder for Kaytrix. He readied a towel to dry.

"I know something happened," Kent said. "I don't know what exactly and I won't pretend to know." He stole a glance at Kaytrix.

Kaytrix nodded silently, content to feel the warmth of the dish between his hands as he dried and stacked it in the cupboard.

Kent abandoned the sink to give him a hug. "We love you, son. Whatever happens, remember that at least," he uttered, tightening his embrace.

Kaytrix returned the hug, lost in his father's tall frame.

Buzz, buzz.

"They are calling me," Kaytrix announced solemnly, disengaging from his father.

"It's okay, son," Kent said, patting his arm. "I won't tell your ma anything. The less she worries about, the better."

"Yes, I agree. Thanks for everything. The cake was delicious."

His father fetched his cloak and handed it to him. "We will see you again," he choked.

Kaytrix took one more look at his sleeping ma and then at his father. "Take care," he uttered softly. It was hard, turning away from the little house he grew up in. He spent his youth chasing a dream of being in the stars. Now all he wanted was to stay home with his family.

Approaching the barn, he activated his comm. "Commander Torex," he grunted as he opened the barn door and readied the drorse to leave.

"Sir, Lieutenant Levro speaking."

"What do you have to report?" Kaytrix asked, swinging himself over the stocky drorse.

"Sir, the engineers have repaired the engine's power coils damaged during the fight. We're half a rotation away from getting the replacement part installed. I am uncertain when the other repairs will be complete."

"Very well, Lieutenant. Thank you for the update. Stand by for further instructions."

"Yes, sir."

Kaytrix rode the drorse through the gate and back onto the drifting road. The wind had died down since he arrived, giving him the silence he needed to think.

If this really was going to be the end of Archaria, if their allies were joining Lord Khelveliz, then his last mission was clear: if they were going down, he was going to give Khelveliz one hell of a fight.

Chapter 16

EVACUATION

It took the council two rotations to consult with the admiral. They took stock of their resources and personnel, and reevaluated if their proposal for an alpha site was achievable. In the end, they decided to proceed with the evacuation. Archaria would move to a world unknown to their allies, a place where they could rebuild. The decision seemed rushed and smacked of weakness. The idea of running away from this fight wasn't what Kaytrix imagined for himself, or for the legacy of Archaria.

Upon reaching their verdict, Karva, Sarneft, and Perseph prepared to address Avsilan and neighboring cities. They gathered in the military training arena to admit their failures and announce their plan to the people.

Kaytrix stood by with the imperial guards while the council gave their announcement, televised on large holo-screens. There was an overwhelming sense of defeat coming from the council. It sickened him. They could have prevented this if only they'd let go of their pride and asked for help in the beginning.

While Kaytrix observed the gathering crowd, a range of emotions from confusion to anger swept across their faces. He had experienced those same emotions over the course of the last half rotation, but none of those emotions were as strong as betrayal.

He turned around to see the councillors, curious if they could sense the crowd as he could. He waited to hear their admittance of the full truth and their explanation of what led to this sudden decision to evacuate.

The council took turns sharing the half-truths of their predicament, their bodies rigid as they stood before the crowd, their faces solemn. They were halfway through their announcement when the crowd erupted into a rage of shouts. The council members scuttled backward out of fear as the civilians pressed the line of imperial guards. The crowd shouted and cried, creating an intense moment. Then the gathering quieted just enough to allow the session to continue.

There was movement among the crowd as more imperial guards took formation between the councillors and the unsettled group. The state of their civilization was apparent in how they needed to use force against their own people.

What the councillors said next was a shock. They explained Archarians within an age range were to be transported first: those just born to those in their early seventies. There was another criterion the council rattled off: those in the Creative and Warrior clans who held positions of power and knowledge, regardless of age, received priority for evacuation.

The crowd erupted, pushing against Kaytrix and the imperial guards. The enraged throng shouted, resisting the council's dictation of their fate. One chant stuck out amid the chaos: a call for new leadership.

It was hard for Kaytrix to watch, but also hold the crowd in check. He lowered his gaze, knowing he had played a part in this. He tightened his fists as anger welled up inside of him. He wasn't alone in his feelings. The crowd's anger and his own were the same. The announcement meant certain civilians could not leave Archaria. Civilians like his parents. It was a cruel decision he and the crowd were victims of.

The crowd's shouts bombarded his ears. Their cries were from anger at change and sacrifice. Yet if the council surrendered to Lord Khelveliz, their screams would be from anger at slavery and annihilation.

As deceptive as they were, the council had tried to make the best decision for their race. It was hard for him to believe that, knowing the truth that they could have prevented this, had it not been for their pride and arrogance.

He listened as the council tried to continue their announcement over the uprising of voices. They shouted, promising to spare those they could. They stressed the need for civilian cooperation, but the crowd pushed against the imperial guards, thirsting for the councillors' blood.

Kaytrix pushed them back, his military instincts kicking in. Their strength was becoming too much. If they pushed through, they would murder the council and create chaos.

Beside him, lit torches stood in their stands. If the imperial guards couldn't keep them back, the fire would. He grabbed a torch and threw it onto the cobblestones at the crowd's feet. The flames spread out before them with the combustible liquid it fed from. The crowd gasped and stepped back, their eyes devilish with the reflection of the fire.

They needed someone other than the council to talk to, someone who understood their pain and frustration. It was hard to relate to a member of the council unaffected by this devastating news.

The crowd took a few steps forward despite the dwindling fire, their shouts gaining in volume again. If Kaytrix was going to do something, now was the time.

"Wait!" he called.

"Get out of the way," a voice demanded.

The crowd ceased yelling to hear the conversation.

Kaytrix held his ground, his hands up. "There is something much worse awaiting us if we do not follow what the councillors are asking." His voice echoed through the outside arena.

"Easy for you to say," another voice blurted. "Your family is from the Warrior clan. They are safe from these orders!"

A chorus of agreeing voices echoed through the arena, threatening his confidence.

"On the contrary, fellow Archarian," he said. He revealed the dull black Farmer clan marking on his forearm and held it up for all to see. "I am from the Farmer clan!"

An audible gasp escaped the crowd at differing intervals.

He shuddered inside. Something he was once ashamed to have had more power than any weapon he ever held.

"My family is not safe from these orders, but none of us will survive what is to come if we do not find the strength to do what is right. Listen to the councillors. Be patient. We are working to save everyone, but we must start somewhere. An uprising will only doom us all. Is that what you want?"

The people's angered faces changed, but instead of showing respect, they showed resentment. Part of the crowd grew silent and dispersed while others stared him down.

He held his ground. This was one battle of many to come. Despite the council's words and promises, leaving their home world would not go as smoothly as they hoped. He remembered his farming days when they separated drorse adults from the babies. There was always a fight. There was always resistance. This was no different. Not only did their leaders turn their backs on their allies, but they did the same to their people. Their poor decisions led them to suffer the consequences.

The angered mob soon emptied the stadium and he turned from the crowd to help one imperial guard to his feet. Others joined in to smother the flames.

The evacuation began soon after the council returned to the safety of the Grand Hall's inner chambers. The crowds left and Kaytrix found a moment to quiet his mind outside the archives.

Inside the room, the crystals were being taken and placed in secure carriers. The future of their race needed every piece of information they could take with them.

He leaned his head back against the wall when his comm activated. He answered it and listened. After a moment, he closed his eyes and sighed.

The admiral instructed him to help with the evacuation until the *Ro'arck's* repairs were complete. After that, he was to aid the blockade. He wasn't sure he was up for it, but he needed to try. He could fight to protect his people, so why not channel that same energy into saving them?

The days were long and grueling. The hardest part was witnessing families refusing to leave each other. He was grateful to help wherever he could but, as he predicted, the evacuation started rough. Civil unrest consumed Archaria.

Despite the unrest, the council continued to hide the truth from the people, forever fearful it could cause more of an outrage. They ignored the topic of new leadership and the growing demand for answers. Their neglect only caused more problems. Now the council fought with its own people to save them.

It was hell.

It was hard to see the repercussions of the council's decisions, and he yearned to return to the *Ro'arck*. He struggled with aiding his people, seeing how ungrateful they were, knowing the allies continued their struggle against Lord Khelveliz alone and without support.

The allies couldn't run and hide. The only places the allies had were their worlds. Their bravery helped fuel his drive to persevere with his tasks.

Chapter 17

THE HUNT

Once the *Narvent* restored the *Ro'arck* to its full battle capacity, Kaytrix received his ultimate mission. The admiral made it clear he was to find and decapitate the evil that had reared its head in the galaxy. If they could defeat the Nevo, nothing could prompt his armies to attack.

Kaytrix and the crew of the *Ro'arck* were alone in this mission. None of the fleet were to join him, their priorities on the remaining ally planets. While not optimal, he still possessed an advantage, one Lord Khelveliz still hadn't exposed: T'vos.

Nat and Tuce also devised a way to track Lord Khelveliz's ship after many trials and errors. Their sensors could now detect the unique signature of the Nevo ship's engines, allowing them to follow him. It was only a matter of discovering a trail and tracking him down.

The allies had speculated the whereabouts of Lord Khelveliz based on his attacks. The planet he was last seen at was Shrovon. It was the only lead they had to work with, and Kaytrix was grateful for the tip.

Kaytrix settled into his command and glanced at T'vos, standing strong at his terminal. It had taken T'vos a while to recuperate after the conflict at Varanus, but he was here now and cleared for duty.

"Sir, there is an incoming communiqué from the Shargan queen," Satki announced, peering at him through her blond bangs.

"Let's see it," he said, nodding his readiness.

The queen appeared in a holographic light before him. "Hello, Commander." She smiled, her turquoise hair floating around her like nebula wisps.

"Hello. Calling to bid us farewell and good luck?" he asked, raising an eyebrow. He knew she had called about T'vos. Even before he boarded the *Ro'arck*, she'd spoken to him about what he couldn't do in battle.

"Remember, T'vos has his limits. If you are both careless . . ."

"Yes, I know. We will be careful," he promised. He didn't want to put T'vos in the same predicament as before.

She nodded. "Very well."

Her communication wisped away into nothingness, revealing the open bridge before him and his crew at their stations. The ship set off, disembarking from the *Narvent*. He browsed through his screen, searching for Shrovon, where they might pick up Lord Khelveliz's trail.

He was beyond ready to begin this mission. After witnessing his planet go through the motions of an evacuation and experiencing the loss and defeat of his council and the members of the alliance, he was determined to hunt Lord Khelveliz down.

And so, the mission of the *Ro'arck* began.

"Set course for Shrovon. Shields at maximum strength and weapons ready," he said, monitoring all systems from his seat.

The *Ro'arck* engaged thrusters and entered the dancing portal of light before them. On the other side, the planet Shrovon lay ahead with her dual moons. The icy world reminded Kaytrix of Archaria, with its dominant cold seasons and short but beautiful warm seasons.

"Anything on the sensors, Kersa?" he asked, rising from his seat to observe the view before him. Several Shrovon ships patroled in the distance.

"Mmm," Kersa said, shaking her head. Her gray eyes observed the screen, lost in concentration. "Yes, I have something. It's several rotations old, but there's an indication of where he may have gone."

"Let's see it."

A holographic display lit the space in front of him, filling the bridge. The blue light showed a series of stars they could jump to and a green line that represented the signal of Lord Khelveliz's ship.

"It looks like he's visiting a world outside the alliance. Jedav," Kaytrix mumbled. "There's nothing there for technology. What could he want from there?" He held his chin as the planet became the center of the display. He read the information they'd categorized on it. Truly, the reason didn't matter. They needed to get there and end this.

"Alright, Nat, take us to Jedav. Drozah, as soon as we exit the portal, I want you targeting his engines so he can't escape. T'vos," he said, looking to him, "are you ready?"

T'vos nodded. His body illuminated and lost mass as he prepared the shields.

They jumped through their portal and arrived at Jedav. The black ship waited for them, its curled form hanging over the planet like a spider with prey in its web.

"Open fire!" Kaytrix barked, tightening his hands into fists.

Their improved missiles flashed across the space between them and struck Lord Khelveliz's ship. Green ripples from the shields surged across the black hull followed by two red eruptions.

"Direct hit, Commander!" Levro exclaimed. "They still have their engines, but we've caused some damage."

"Continue firing!"

Lord Khelveliz's ship moved as two more of their missiles raced to intercept him. The black ship's main cannon turned in their direction. Kaytrix held his breath as two enormous blasts flew their way.

The *Ro'arck* swerved, thanks to Nat's guidance, and missed one of the two blasts. Two more red eruptions from their missiles burned the surface of the Nevo ship.

"We've damaged a sub-light engine," roared Tuce.

"He's picking up speed," warned Nat. "We've pissed him off."

Kaytrix sat back down as Nat gained proximity to the enemy ship. At last, they were making progress. If they could win this battle, there would be no need to evacuate Archaria, and they could help fallen worlds fight for their freedom.

"Keep targeting him. He can't get away this time," he growled.

Another blast from Lord Khelveliz zoomed toward them, this time hitting their shields from atop as their ship passed below.

A yellow light danced on their faces before disappearing, the system stabilized by Tuce's quick hands.

"Come about and continue fire," Kaytrix said. The *Ro'arck* made a one-hundred-eighty-degree turn. Now they were chasing Lord Khelveliz. The moment was surreal.

"Sir, he's jumping to another planet," Nat said from the cockpit.

Anxiety knotted Kaytrix's stomach. Lord Khelveliz couldn't get away. Those days were over. Now they could track him. "Follow him to wherever he goes next. There's nowhere in the galaxy he can hide."

The black ship disappeared and shortly after, they arrived at the same destination, a small planet that was the birthplace of this nightmare: O'ber. The ships from their destroyed fleet ages ago were being reconstructed into new vessels. Masses of them mangled together, taking on a new hideous shape and meaning.

Kaytrix's blood boiled at the reminder of the immense loss Archaria suffered on this planet. Their lives taken and shaped into something purely evil. It was downright perverted.

"Sir, Lord Khelveliz is aware of our presence. He's targeting us," Levro announced, his voice steady.

"Sir," said Kersa, her jaw dropping. "I am detecting seven new Nevo ships."

Kaytrix understood her bewilderment. All this time, they had assumed there were only two ships. But his sensors revealed what was happening to the old Archarian ships. They were recreating them as their own. He gazed at the wreckage of the other ships and a stabbing pain shot through him.

"Target his ship. Destroy his primary weapon and engines," he growled. "Drozah, destroy those abominations while you're at it. Fallen soldiers and ships are not to be disrespected in such a way."

Drozah nodded. The forward section of ship turrets let loose a sea of fire. The closest Nevo ship fell apart within moments, its frail structure not yet shielded. They targeted the next one in range, and it fell apart within the same timeframe.

A sudden blast struck the *Ro'arck*. Systems flashed messages fervently across his screen. Kaytrix steadied himself, grasping his terminal.

Through the viewport, he spotted Lord Khelveliz's ship approaching.

"Sir, that was a concentrated shot. He's trying to overload our shields," Tuce warned.

Kaytrix turned to gaze at T'vos, but the Shargan remained steadfast in his position with no sign of struggling, yet. "T'vos, talk to me. What should we do?"

T'vos turned his head toward him. "I recommend we avoid that kind of fire as much as we can. Concentrated energy is harder for me to process and repurpose, taking longer each time to put back into the shields."

"Alright, we'll be careful. Let's continue with our attack."

The *Ro'arck* received another two blasts from a different Nevo ship, this one no longer a heap of scrap. Then another fired on them. Three ships bombarded their shields.

T'vos groaned, his body already reaching its limitations. They had to abort. Here they were, so close to finishing this, to be once again forced to leave. Only this time, they could come back and finish the job when T'vos was ready.

Kaytrix prepared to give the order to leave when Lord Khelveliz's ship moved off from the skirmish and jumped through a portal.

Should they still abort? The last thing he wanted was to endanger T'vos's life.

The Shargan nodded his head. "I'm . . . fine," he struggled to say.

"Follow him," Kaytrix hissed.

The *Ro'arck* followed the Nevo lord's ship only to face an armada of Varanus and various other vessels on the other side. A stillness consumed the bridge. He'd never seen so many ships before.

"S-sir," Satki said, her lip quivering. "Lord Khelveliz is hailing us."

Kaytrix sighed. If it weren't for this apparent stalemate, he'd skip the conversation and destroy the ship, but the other vessels hindered their plan. Lord Khelveliz would not die today.

He sat down. "Put it up."

Lord Khelveliz appeared in the pulsing holographic blue light. "Commander Torex," he hissed. "So, you can track my ship. Not much of an advantage, is it?"

Kaytrix swallowed. This predicament was evidence enough. If only there were five more *Ro'arck's* and Shargans, this scenario would play out differently.

"Depends on how you look at it," he fired back. "Who's saying I don't go back to O'ber and destroy the rest of those abominations you call ships?"

Lord Khelveliz slammed his fist onto his command console. "Wouldn't matter if you did," he spat. "The only reason you're still breathing is because I want something from *you*."

Kaytrix raised his eyebrows. "Oh, yeah? Let me guess. My surrender?" He scoffed.

Khelveliz's fist tightened. The sound of metal scratching against itself grated Kaytrix's ears, making his skin crawl.

"The Shargan," Khelveliz breathed impatiently.

Kaytrix's heart froze. How did he know . . . ? He remembered Karva's confession about mission 3199: *our secrets, our allies, our weaknesses . . . stolen and distorted.*

So, Lord Khelveliz had pieced together how they could stand against him in battle. He must know about the Shargans' abilities, but there was no way he was surrendering T'vos. He motioned with his hands toward Levro to ready a portal to leave. They couldn't survive another barrage.

"I'd rather die," he declared.

Lord Khelveliz screeched, throwing his head back to release the awful noise.

"Now!" Kaytrix called, ending the communication.

Nat piloted the *Ro'arck* below the Varanus ships and through a portal to home.

A sigh of relief swept through the crew, and they settled at their stations. The *Ro'arck* floated safely on the other side of the portal, the view of Archaria and the *Narvent* before them.

Kaytrix was glad they made it back, but now Lord Khelveliz knew their tactic. Next time, he could count on Lord Khelveliz waiting for him. They would wait a rotation, allowing Lord Khelveliz to move about, and give T'vos the chance to recuperate. If they had to fight with a hit-and-run strategy, then they would. While not the best plan, it was the only thing that could keep T'vos safe and the *Ro'arck* in one piece.

"Sir, the admiral is calling," advised Satki.

Kaytrix reached to activate the comm on his terminal. "Commander Torex," he answered.

"Commander, what's your status?"

He took in a breath, preparing to bring the admiral up to speed. If the admiral expected the Nevo lord to be found and destroyed, then he was optimistic.

"Sir, we're giving T'vos a rotation before we pursue the enemy again."

The admiral cleared his throat. "I'm afraid that will have to wait. I need you to divert from your current mission and aid the Shrovons. They've reported a group of Varanus ships in their orbit and need help to push them back. We can't let them fall to the enemy."

"Yes, Admiral. We will leave right away. Commander Torex, out."

When he broke off the communication, his crew stared at him from their terminals. He could tell they were leery about heading back out so soon, but they needed to be out there fighting, not sitting docked here.

"Come on, crew, on to Shrovon," he said, clapping his hands together. He checked in with each of the crew members. Everyone stood ready, but the toll this battle was having on them was obvious. The fresh plump faces from their first flight together were weary and worn soldiers now. He desired nothing more than to end this, but sacrifices needed to be made.

The *Ro'arck* arrived at Shrovon to a scene of intense orbital warfare. Blasts pounded the opposition while the defense received an intense beating in return. Kaytrix could see on his screen that the Shrovon vessels were holding their own. Their ships were smaller, but the alloy used to create their ships was strong. Even Archarian vessels weren't made as well as a Shrovon's ship.

"You know the drill, people. Let's get in and out with minimal damage," he said as he patrolled the bridge.

The crew set to work, and the focus of the battle shifted. The Varanus attacked, pounding the *Ro'arck's* shields with great ferocity. Kaytrix's viewport filled with the forward fire they received, an ominous shift of orange and blue light dancing across their faces. The shields rippled in a wavelike motion, preventing anything from getting through.

They returned fire and, like he suspected, the Nevo outfitted these Varanus ships with the new shields. Like they discovered before, this battle would take time unless they used their new but limited missiles.

The last thing he wanted was to use all their missiles only to have Lord Khelveliz arrive with them unable to defend themselves. They would have to make do with their standard weapons.

Moments passed, then several ships broke off from the assault. What were they up to now? Kaytrix activated his screen. Three of the ships were heading back to Shrovon, only they weren't targeting the Shrovon starships—they were targeting the planet.

Orange energy ripped from the barrels of their guns. The large cannon fire penetrated the atmosphere and gouged the planet, destroying cities and massacring millions of Shrovon civilians.

So, the Varanus didn't perceive Archarians as a threat anymore? He admitted the battle was a bit of a stalemate, each of them with powerful shields and weapons not strong enough to penetrate. But he couldn't stand here and wait for millions to be destroyed. They had to do something.

"T'vos! I hate to ask you this," he said, "but we need to protect Shrovon. Switch to weapons."

T'vos nodded and squared his broad shoulders. The armor of his uniform shifted, and with it the surrounding energy wisped and pulsed.

"Targeting the enemy ships in orbit," he announced.

The forward guns swiveled and fired. The empowered weapons pierced through the shields and destroyed the Varanus' forward systems, but the Varanus continued their attack despite their damage.

Kaytrix was afraid this would happen. To protect the planet, they would have to destroy the Varanus vessels. Surrender wasn't an option.

The *Ro'arck's* shields continued to hold while T'vos attacked the enemy ships. The Shrovon starships also aided in the attack, teaming up to target the weakening vessels. In moments, the Varanus attack was over, their ships either destroyed or neutralized.

Kaytrix wiped the sweat from his brow, ecstatic at their win. "Great job, everyone," he whooped.

A siren for proximity wailed. Kersa frantically searched her terminal for the source of the warning.

"Sir, six Varanus ships are inbound."

The vessels approached like hunters stalking prey, slow and steady and inciting the same fear. The question wasn't if the Archarians could protect Shrovon. The question was, how long could they protect Shrovon?

Kaytrix sat back down. Their systems were still in good standing.

"Let's show them what we can do. Nat, evasive tactics while T'vos powers the guns," he ordered.

They launched their attack, destroying the guns on the first vessel and damaging the shield generators on the other two. Three vessels charged past them for the planet, attacking them and the Shrovon ships in orbit.

"Don't let them get through," he called as he observed his screens. The three vessels heading for the planet were a different class of ship: dropships. A surge of urgency rose through him. They had to stop the dropships from dropping their cargo. He couldn't allow Varanus soldiers to be released onto the planet.

"T'vos, we need to destroy those dropships!"

"On it, Commander. Targeting them now."

The dropships raged closer to orbit, their shields blazing as they entered the atmosphere. They needed to hurry. Varanus fighters emerged from their hangars and created a formation above the descending ships.

The *Ro'arck's* attack hit the fighters, leaving the enemy dropships intact. They were using their own fighters as an external shield to barricade their attack.

"We've disabled the first three ships, sir," reported Levro. "Just the dropships now!"

T'vos grunted and Kaytrix turned to see the Shargan quivering from the strain. "Tell the Shrovon ships to back off," he growled. "They don't want to get hit by this."

Before Kaytrix could object, Satki was relaying the order, and T'vos was humming again.

"No, T'vos, there's another way!" he yelled. It was too late. T'vos was already gathering the power of the ship to focus into the intense beam of energy he had used at the Varanus planet—the same tactic that took him out of action for several rotations.

The beam of energy cut through the space between them, incinerating the Varanus dropships.

Through the viewport, carcasses of ships floated down through the atmosphere and burned.

"Power has returned to all systems, Commander," Levro said, turning to him. "We have destroyed all enemy craft. For now," he added with a weary look.

Kaytrix nodded his thanks and turned to T'vos. The Shargan was barely standing, holding himself up. His armor appeared dull. The magical wisps that once floated around his vibrant body were gone, as if the strenuous action drained his life force.

T'vos nodded once. "We did it," he said.

Kaytrix shook his head. "No, you did it, T'vos." He couldn't believe he'd risked his own life yet again to serve and protect.

"Sir," said Satki.

Kaytrix flinched. He was beginning to associate the sound of her voice with the impending scratch of Lord Khelveliz's voice.

"Go ahead, Satki."

She nodded, her bangs fluttering as she pressed some buttons. "The Shrovon are patching in a message for us from Queen Rayla."

His heart stopped and he feared what she might say. "What's the message?"

Satki swallowed before relaying the message. "She says T'vos must return to their home world."

There it was. The thing he'd feared she would say. He turned to T'vos. "Time for you to go home, champion. You've done your job."

T'vos forced himself to stand, his height surpassing Kaytrix's by a head. "We aren't done yet. My mission was to aid you in destroying Lord Khelveliz."

"No, my friend," he said. "That time has come and gone. The queen requests your presence home. And if I know anything, it's that she is always right."

T'vos chuckled, a deep and pulsing sound with his ventilator. "This is true. I promise I will return as soon as I can aid you."

Kaytrix clasped his shoulder. "We've got this. With our improved missiles and tracking system, we will have Lord Khelveliz in no time." He winked. T'vos was being stubborn. Of course, he needed him for their mission, but he had lost enough lives. Tracking Lord Khelveliz was something they could do on their own. T'vos needed his rest.

"Come, I'll walk you to the hangar. From there you can travel to Shrovon and use their arkross to get home."

T'vos stood reluctantly at his station, but he finally let go of the terminal and joined Kaytrix in the lift.

The ride down to the hangar was quiet. Kaytrix hadn't been down here since he lost Mac, and now he was losing T'vos. This war caused nothing but loss.

When they reached the hangar, T'vos turned to him. "Commander Torex, I am glad I got the chance to fight with you. It's been many solar rotations since I've experienced such exhilaration."

Kaytrix reflected on their journey together as they entered the hangar. "It was an honor, T'vos." He turned to look at him and saluted.

T'vos's head tilted, a motion Kaytrix was slowly learning meant a different range of emotions. "I'll see you again, Torex."

The Shargan entered the ship and prepared to take off, leaving Kaytrix standing alone.

Chapter 18

THREATS

When the *Ro'arck* arrived at the *Narvent*, Kaytrix was grateful. Their last mission was an immense success, but it was important they restock their improved missiles and get underway at once. Time was not on his side.

The *Ro'arck* drew nearer to the gray supply docking port of the *Narvent* and finished its docking sequence. He drew his focus away from his display and ran his hand through his hair, a wave of exhaustion overcoming him. The last few rotations were taking their toll on him and his crew.

He glanced to the void tech specialist station. Without T'vos aboard, and no one to take his place, they were prime targets for Lord Khelveliz. It was terrible timing.

He tore his gaze away to overlook the *Ro'arck*'s systems as they readied to receive the missiles from the *Narvent*. He could hear Lieutenant Levro briefly speaking with the lead operator. They were ready to begin the transfer.

Drozah stood from his seat at the weapons terminal. "I'm going to help load the missiles," he said, wiping a hand across his nose.

Drozah's face was red as he walked to the lift. Since the council had announced the plan of an alpha site, everyone was on pins and needles. The war had spent his crew's energy, and now they bore emotional weight. No one knew if their families were going to make it to the alpha site or not.

War takes everything from a person, even those moments of peace, he thought. It had been days since any of them could catch a moment of silence.

He focused on Nat as an exhausted sigh left her.

"I am having a nap," she grumbled, resting her head on her folded arms.

"Make it quick," he teased.

"Oh, no way, I think I could sleep for a thousand solar rotations." She yawned again.

Kaytrix smiled. "I'd miss you."

Her head shot up from her folded arms and she turned to look at him. "I guess I'd miss you too," she admitted. "But right now, I'm sleeping." She plopped her head back down.

He chuckled. "Good, I don't need a cranky pilot." A muffled giggle came from her and then silence.

He had no sooner spoke when a hail from the surface blipped on the communication screen.

"Sir, it's the council hailing us," Satki said.

"Open the channel." He thumbed the underside of his clasp, fidgeting with it and tried not to project what the message could be.

Karva Norda's face appeared in the holographic light. "Commander Torex. There have been recent developments we need to discuss." His solemn tone alarmed Kaytrix.

"Of course, councillor. What's going on?"

"While you were defending the Shrovon planet, Archaria received an urgent message from the King of Cordabo requesting the *Ro'arck*'s immediate aid."

This wasn't the update he was expecting to hear. They'd already been gone a full rotation—that was three rotations for Cordabo. "We will head out as soon as possible, councillor."

Hearing of Cordabo's need made him think Lord Khelveliz planned the fight at Shrovon to keep him busy. Whether or not that was the intention, it had worked.

Karva blinked and hung his head when Perseph stepped into the hologram.

"It's too late, Commander. Just as you arrived, we received another message."

There was a pause and Perseph swallowed. Kaytrix wasn't sure he was going to like what he was going to say next.

Karva pulled at his collar and wiped his forehead. "Commander, it isn't favorable news. The Cordabo have fallen. The king told me Lord Khelveliz wanted to send us a message . . ." Karva blinked away tears.

It was harsher news than he anticipated, and the thought sickened him. Another failure. "What's the message?" He gritted his teeth, bracing himself.

Karva choked on his words as he spoke. "Lord Khelveliz is coming for Archaria. He said to 'prepare to burn.'"

Kaytrix's blood boiled, enraged at Lord Khelveliz's taunt. Was this the reason the Nevo lord was not present in their last battle? Had he conquered Cordabo to prepare an attack against Archaria?

"We are far from evacuating everyone pre-selected," Karva said. "It will take several more rotations that we don't have. We need the entire fleet to return and provide protection and transport for Archaria."

Kaytrix couldn't believe it was coming to this: abandoning their allies to leave their home. Was this how their legacy ended? He couldn't imagine living a life where he fled the face of battle, abandoning his allies. A life where Lord Khelveliz got the last laugh.

"We can't recall those ships! Our allies depend on us for protection and support. The Shargans, too. We can't abandon them." There must be something they could do.

"There's no other way, Commander." Karva took a breath. "It's unfortunate it has come to this."

Kaytrix scowled. "Yes, it is." His fists tightened as all his battles with the allies and T'vos flashed before his eyes. All along, they planned to evacuate. Now that they were following through with abandoning the alliance, he never anticipated how it would feel. An emptiness consumed him. Was all of it for nothing?

"How much time do you think we have, Commander?" Perseph asked.

"I am not sure. Knowing Lord Khelveliz, he will want a challenge and we'll give him one."

Karva nodded. "Admiral Ackon will be in touch to begin the preparations."

The communication ended, and in its wake, various Archarian starships arrived through portals. While some ships took formation around their planet, others approached the *Narvent* to dock.

"How will the alliance ever forgive our race for abandoning them?" he uttered to himself sadly. "Satki, let me speak to the crew." There was no need to lose more lives.

"You are good to go, sir," Satki said.

"Crew of the *Ro'arck*," he said, his voice quivering. He grunted, clearing his throat as Drozah appeared on the bridge. "I have just received word that Archaria is abandoning our allies to defend our home world and the efforts to leave to the alpha site. As commander, I am relieving you of duty. If you are not a bridge officer or stationed at a crucial terminal, evacuate to the *Narvent,* and proceed to the surface. You have served me and the Archarian race with bravery and honor. Thank you. Peace to you all."

He nodded for Satki to end the announcement. Asking the officers to stay was asking them to sacrifice their lives. Everyone aboard the *Ro'arck* deserved to continue to live.

He faced the bridge and spoke when Nat cut him off.

"Don't even think of asking us to step down." Her burgundy hair glistened in the light from the ship. "We're here with you to the end." She strapped herself into her seat. "I am staying right where I am."

Drozah crossed his arms and huffed. "Let's show this asshole what we're made of," he growled.

"I can't imagine running now, Commander," Levro said. "Not when our call to duty has never been stronger."

Kaytrix acknowledged their bravery, grateful for their commitment. "Very well, let's get to work." He grimaced after a moment as they turned from him and initiated appropriate preparations. He hoped they had considered it, at least.

"So, what's the plan?" Nat asked, turning to look at him, her brown eyes soft.

"Wait for Khelveliz to arrive and kick his ass. Hopefully." Kaytrix half smiled. The likelihood of that happening was slim.

Nat and Drozah chuckled with him. Deep within, he struggled to acknowledge if this was their last mission together. With T'vos gone, they didn't stand half a chance, leaving little room for hope.

The armies of Lord Khelveliz were coming for them. And, with the last of their forces pulled from their allies, no one was coming to save them.

"Nat, once the crew has left, lets join the other starships. We will form the mountain formation, as a tribute to our world. We're to hold the line at all costs."

"Affirmative, Commander." Nat nodded.

Kaytrix caught Drozah searching his face.

"You better talk to your ma and father," Drozah blurted, surprising him.

"Duty first," he said. "You should contact your family, Drozah. When you find a moment."

Drozah nodded.

It was a thoughtful idea, to give any remaining crew the opportunity to say a last goodbye. They deserved that much, and as a commander, he owed them that much.

It took time for the crew to board the *Narvent*. Those moments allowed them to get all their missiles into the warhead chamber where a computerized system autoloaded the arms to the gunports needing ammunition.

Kaytrix focused on Nat in the pilot's seat. She was browsing systems, no doubt. "Nat," he addressed her, his tone soft.

She turned to peer at him, the motion difficult in her seat. "Yes, Commander?"

"You should call your family before we join formation," he said, his eyes resting on the soft contours of her face.

Nat smiled. "Thank you, Commander, I will."

Nat turned in her seat and arranged the call. In seconds, she connected to her parents. He found it difficult to hear them weep, begging her to come home and be with them. To hear Nat choke on her words, the strain in her voice as she chose duty over her own needs, both hurt and made him proud of her. The call ended in phrases of farewells, love, and the hope of seeing each other again.

Nat removed her headgear to cradle her face and weep silently.

It was the hardest thing a person could do—to promise something you weren't sure of yourself. He had a compelling desire to say something comforting, but he didn't know how. He faced the same path, and now it was his turn.

"Communications Officer, if you could connect me to the Torex household," he said, settling in his seat.

"Connection made," Satki said.

"Hello?" His father's voice came through the speakers in confusion, his face squinting at the screen.

Kaytrix switched on a light, forgetting the *Ro'arck*'s bridge was naturally dim for the use of their holographic screens.

"There you are!" His father's voice rang happily.

"Hey, how are you?" Kaytrix choked out. The conversation was just starting and already it was getting tough.

"The question is, how are you, my boy? Ma's doing okay. She still has her days, but she's not any worse. I'm fine but getting old." He laughed. "Are you coming home? I hope that is why you are calling. I just made dessert."

He smiled, his face touching the screen. "Ahna, come here, Kaytrix is on the screen."

Kaytrix's throat tightened, seizing, betraying him when he needed it the most. He had much he wished to say. So much he regretted not saying sooner.

"I . . . I am afraid not. You and Ma might want to pack and head to the city for a transport," he said.

His father stared at him in confusion. "What do you mean, son? Everything here is fine."

Kaytrix took in a slow breath. "Didn't you hear? The council addressed the cities. The alliance disbanded, and an enemy is coming to face our fleet." He swallowed.

His eyes left his father's face to see his ma join them. He smiled. She appeared in good health since his last visit.

"Is that my son spewing doomsday nonsense?" She stood beside her husband and squinted at the screen. "There's my boy!" Ahna exclaimed happily. "You beat this evil and come home. We miss you, and the dessert is getting cold."

Kaytrix smiled as tears threatened to breach his eyes. His parents didn't understand the gravity of the situation. "Pack important items we might not have access to for a while and head for the city right away," he said.

His parents' smiles faded, and confusion entered their eyes. The seriousness of their circumstances was sinking in.

"Look, son. Your ma is better but not well. To get caught up in a panic . . ." his voice drifted. "If what you say is true, I'd prefer to spend my last moments holding her," Kent said. "I hope you can understand that."

Kaytrix nodded and a single tear broke free from his eye. "I love you both," he choked out through clenched teeth. He struggled to be brave, to be strong when they needed him to be. But how could he remember to be the man he grew into when his parents reminded him of the small child he was inside?

"We love you, Kaytrix, and we are so proud of the man you have become." It was his father's turn to choke up.

His ma followed. "Sweetheart, just do your best out there, okay? We love you and will think of you." She smiled, tears streaking her face as she blew a kiss.

"I guess I'll have to eat your portion of the dessert." Kent laughed, wiping a tear away with his rough, aged hands.

Kaytrix chortled. "I have to go now."

They nodded and hugged each other, their smiles replaced by sorrow. "Peace be with you," his father rasped in hopefulness.

"Peace be with you," Kaytrix echoed.

The communication ended and he composed himself, letting out a breath he'd been holding.

"They sound at peace," Nat smiled. "I remember your ma's dessert well," she continued fondly. "Drozah always had to have the biggest piece when we visited!" She laughed, wiping her eyes.

He laughed too, his face red. "I can't believe you remember that," he admitted.

Nat looked insulted. "Of course! How could anyone forget your ma's baking?" She winked.

Drozah returned to the command bridge in that moment, his face red from tears. He had called his family privately.

He sniffed. "What'd I miss?" he asked, clearing his throat as if everything was normal.

"Just reminiscing about how you *always* got the biggest piece of my ma's dessert." Kaytrix chuckled.

"Hey," Nat exclaimed. "Maybe that is how you got so tall?"

Drozah scowled as Kaytrix and Nat laughed. Then he laughed too.

"What can I say, your ma's dessert was delicious," he admitted, smiling at the delightful memory. "And you were so scrawny, someone had to eat the biggest piece!"

Kaytrix continued to laugh with his friends, and, for a moment, peace replaced the pressures of war.

Chapter 19

THE LAST STAND

The first stage of the Archarian evacuation was complete. The pre-selected Archarians had arrived at the alpha site, and now the council could prepare the remaining civilians for off-world transport.

A sigh of relief swept through the *Ro'arck's* command bridge as Kaytrix and his crew watched the announcement. There was hope of once again seeing their families.

He allowed himself to think of the future struggles awaiting his race. Even with the many supplies for their new life, their greatest issue was restarting. Everything they designed came from the unique world that was their home. Moving to another planet meant discovering everything all over again.

He monitored his screens, one displaying the Archarian fleet in formation, the other the progress of the starships leaving. Where was Lord Khelveliz? It had been four planetary rotations with no sign of or further threats from him.

As time passed, he allowed himself to relax. He inquired of T'vos, but the queen reported he wasn't any better. She promised he'd return to help them as soon as he could. He hoped it was before Lord Khelveliz arrived.

With the extra time to reflect, he thought about the allies. No doubt, they had shared Archaria's location with Lord Khelveliz to spare themselves his wrath. So, if he knew where they were, why wait and announce his plan to attack? Was his hate toward them so severe that he wanted the battle to drag out? He couldn't be sure.

Something else burned in his mind. What had happened before the war had reached this crucial point? The secretive conversation of the council, the restricted mission files . . . something wasn't adding up. Especially surrounding mission 3199, and he still didn't know what happened on mission 3200.

The *Ro'arck's* bridge hummed with the murmurs of the crew and the occasional beep from a console. Kaytrix sat in his chair under the dim lights, peering out the viewport to the space before him. He glanced at the holographic screens to his left. No sign of the enemy.

He recalled his trip to the archive. There had to be more to the old mission reports. The question was, would the leaders of Archaria tell him? He hailed the surface, where the councillors and admirals monitored the evacuation in the Grand Tower.

"Hello, Commander Torex. What is your status?" Karva Norda answered. His voice was calm. Nothing like rotations prior. Beside him sat Admiral Ackon, his gaze focused elsewhere. He didn't see Perseph or Sarneft.

Kaytrix took in a breath. "The ships are moving along steady. Something has been bothering me, though. I thought you could help?" he asked, watching the councillor's response.

"A medical officer could aid you, Commander," Karva suggested, his gaze focused elsewhere.

"No, not in this instance," Kaytrix responded.

This time, Admiral Ackon looked his way.

Karva turned his attention onto him. "Very well. What is it?"

"What else happened during mission 3200?" Kaytrix asked. He scrutinized the aged Archarians before him, waiting.

Ackon's face soured, anger in his eyes. "That was merely an update. Now is not the time to dredge up the past," he retorted before Karva could reply.

Karva's nostrils flared, his eyes widening. Did he think Kaytrix would forget about everything? He resisted speaking, watching Karva. If anyone could give away the truth, it would be him, but could he?

Karva's shoulders dropped, and he looked to Ackon seated beside him. "We need to tell him." He sighed, catching both Kaytrix and the admiral by surprise.

"There's no point!" Ackon argued, whirling to scowl at Karva.

"The man may die protecting the future of our race," Karva stated, abruptly rising from his seat. "He deserves to know!"

There was a pause, and a chill traveled up Kaytrix's spine to the nape of his neck. Another quick glance at his screens confirmed there was no sign of enemy ships.

"It doesn't matter now. The truth won't change anything," Admiral Ackon retorted, and turned his attention back to his screen.

Karva sat back down and met Kaytrix's gaze, shaking his head. "We had planned another mission, but there's a reason we left the report blank in the archives," Karva said.

Kaytrix swallowed.

"The council at the time felt threatened by what the Nevo race were capable of, so we came up with a plan to eliminate the problem."

Kaytrix's heartbeat sped.

Karva lowered his gaze and then said, "We captured one of the Nevo on O'ber and interrogated him. We learned they came from another planet, Kohmitz, so we sent bombers there. The pilots' orders were to drop every bomb they had."

Kaytrix shook his head. He clenched his jaw as heat rose throughout his body. He was surprised that he felt angry—not at Khelveliz, but at his own people. No wonder Lord Khelveliz had it out for them, why he had accused them of being murderers. And in Kaytrix's ignorance, he had only stoked the flame.

What this mission revealed was how far the Archarians had strayed from their true purpose of pursuing peace, truth, and unity.

He relaxed his fists and let his breath out. "You owe the people of Archaria the truth, councillor. What's the point of continuing to exist if all we stand for is lies and deceit?"

After he ended the communication, his crew looked at him. Everyone had overheard the exchange, their harsh facial lines and rigid forms telling him exactly what they were feeling: shock and disgust. He couldn't let them face a battle with a soured mood. Their fight had to be pure and for the right reasons.

"Despite the decisions of others that brought us here, we need to continue to fight for the innocent civilians of Archaria. For our families, for the people who do not know this atrocity happened."

Levro slowly nodded his head, but the conversation had clearly affected the young man. His face was a crisp red, his hold on his terminal so tight, his knuckles were white.

Kaytrix understood those feelings all too well, but it was too late to dwell on things they couldn't change. The enemy was coming, and they needed to be ready.

"I can't believe . . ." Levro muttered. "Do we deserve this?" he asked, his eyes welling with tears of rage. "Do we deserve what's coming?"

Kaytrix stood from his chair and approached Levro. As he placed a hand on his shoulder, he said, "I learned the hard way that every action has a reaction. Whether or not it is just is left to perception. Defending ourselves is a reaction to Lord Khelveliz's attack, and in doing so we protect the innocent."

Levro wiped away his tears gruffly and sniffed. "Yes, sir. We fight for the innocent."

Kaytrix left his side to see Nat in her pilot seat looking back at him. She gave a single nod and smiled before turning back to her controls.

There was a sudden wail from Tuce's station. "Commander!" Tuce's voice broke out across the bridge. "Multiple ships have appeared on our sensors!"

Kaytrix snapped to attention. Several ships appeared through hyperspace portals and joined the formation in front of their fleet. Most of the ships were Varanus, a few he recognized as previous allies. It was a twist to his gut he'd never experienced. Among them were several Nevo ships, but Lord Khelveliz was absent.

"Status?" Kaytrix asked.

"They are positioning themselves outside weapons' range, sir," Kersa said.

"Make sure our fleet remains in formation. We can't allow them to break us apart," Kaytrix said.

He focused his attention on the gathering enemy fleet before him. The enemy ships had moved into their formation and now appeared to wait for the command to strike. This was the first time any of Khelveliz's forces had faced the might of the Archarians at once.

His upper lip twitched. He'd anticipated this battle for many rotations. Part of him couldn't wait to fight. The other part of him reveled knowing that his race would survive, despite Lord Khelveliz's attempts to destroy them.

He exhaled impatiently. After losing so many people, having entire fleets destroyed and their allies conquered or turned against them, this is where it ended—with the last stand. Archarian numbers paled in comparison to Lord Khelveliz's fleet, but their starships were capable. Despite that fact, Kaytrix vowed to fight until the end, to make every breath count.

He took in the moment. The dim bridge deck, the contours of the ship's inner panels, the lights that ran along the seams of the walls, the floating holo-screens that lit the faces of a crew he was proud to serve with. Every inch of this conflict had, in a way, become a dream come true. Though the missions and hard choices weren't something we would have chosen for himself, they helped shape him into the commander he'd become.

A flash of hyperspace light diverted his attention. There, to the left of the fleet, the fiercest of Nevo ships poised like a viper ready to strike. It was Lord Khelveliz.

Before Kaytrix had time to assess his sudden arrival, the communications terminal beeped.

"It's Lord Khelveliz, sir," Satki reported in a dry tone.

The crew had learned what to expect next.

"Open the channel," he said calmly with a nod. He waited until Lord Khelveliz appeared before him in the blue light of the hologram. The Nevo lowered his hood, and a dim light above exposed the intricate layers of metal fashioned to his skin. His green eyes burned bright. Was it anger or lust for the fight?

Seeing his enemy before this major battle brought many feelings to the surface: anger, grief, betrayal. But the most predominant feeling was the fear of failure.

"Impressive fleet you have, Commander Torex. It's a shame it won't be enough to stop me," Lord Khelveliz hissed.

Kaytrix ignored the comment. "Why don't we settle this alone, just you and me?" he offered, crossing his arms. "Winner decides the fate of the loser."

"Now where's the fun in that?" the Nevo lord spat. "Do you have any regrets, Commander? It's unfortunate." He paused, holding his metal-fanged chin. "The only regret I have is being unable to hear you scream as you die . . ."

Kaytrix flinched. Khelveliz had struck a chord. Now it was his turn.

"I know why you are here, Lord Khelveliz. I know what you've gone through—the pain, the loss, I can't imagine—"

"Enough," Lord Khelveliz roared. "What you've done is unforgiveable. The only way to pay for blood is with blood. Your world will burn, Torex, and there is nothing you can do—"

Kaytrix punched his terminal, ending the conversation. He didn't need to waste more time.

"All ships, prepare to open fire," he spoke into a shared comm. "Aim for the Nevo ships first. With them out of the picture, we can try to appeal to our old allies."

"You don't have to tell me twice!" Drozah roared.

This was it. He was facing Lord Khelveliz for the last time. There was peace to this, and regret. He wanted more time to do the things that really mattered in his life, like telling Nat how she made him feel.

"Target the Varanus shield generators with our new missiles. That way we can use regular weapons to fend them off," he advised.

The enemy horde broke apart. Several of them attacked his fleet, while others tried to blaze past them. Anti-air turrets on the surface destroyed those who made it near the planet.

"Keep them from getting through!" Kaytrix ordered, observing the battle. So far, the Nevo ships remained out of the fight, letting the others pave the way with their lives.

In moments, the battlefield was a mass of ships, strewn over and above each other. It was obvious the enemy possessed the stronger army. With several conquered worlds of technology under their command, the enemy commanded ships more expendable than his own.

Starships from the Archarian fleet held their ground against the larger fleet, their age and lack of advancement a harsh reminder of the mistakes the council had made.

Kaytrix noted that a section of the formation was weakening, the ship positioned there taking fire from multiple ships.

"Have the *Ro'arck* move in to shield the sister ship from fire!" he barked. He stood to pace the bridge. Sitting idle in his chair wasn't helping his ability to focus on the battle.

"Yes, Commander," Nat said.

Another vessel replaced their position in the blockade to keep it strong. As they rushed to intercept the barrage of weapons fire, a reading of the ship they were going to protect popped up on a screen.

"They have extensive damage. The Varanus are relentless in their attack," Levro said. "Sir, we're too late."

Red lines pulsed on the ship's readouts. They lost their shields and engines, and life support was critical. The Archarian ship fell toward the planet as escape pods jettisoned into space. The ship crumbled and broke apart as the planet drew her into its fiery atmosphere.

Their first loss, and so soon. Kaytrix whirled to view one of Drozah's displays. "Destroy that Varanus ship!" he ordered, a vein in his neck pulsing.

The Varanus starship succumbed to the advanced weaponry of the *Ro'arck*, exploding within moments of being attacked.

"The blockade has destroyed several Varanus ships," Levro announced over the chaos.

Kaytrix welcomed the news. With the Varanus ship destroyed, he could refocus on the larger battle at hand.

One Nevo ship remained plus Lord Khelveliz's vessel, but his fleet had sustained heavy losses. If the Archarians couldn't be as tactful as before, they could lose more than this battle. It was essential that the passenger ships and the *Narvent* stay operating without taking fire.

"Keep on them, crew!" Kaytrix encouraged.

Just as he spoke, a transport ship exploded behind the safety of the blockade, its precious cargo now lost, frozen in the coldness of space. The sudden destruction stopped him mid-pace. He assessed their loss when out of his right eye, he caught the ghostly green weapons fire of the Nevo streaking across space in front of their viewport.

His eyes followed it, and a sick feeling of dread twisted his stomach. The weapons pelted the *Narvent.* Multiple explosions erupted throughout the station, and a chain reaction resulted, traveling the arms of the station until it reached the dome, shattering the glass.

His jaw tightened and a wail built in his chest. He clenched his teeth tighter to keep it in as the station fell apart. He glared at Lord Khelveliz, who was lingering above the battlefield. Until this point in time, he had abstained from fighting as if absorbing the scene of death before him as a pleasing aroma. Guess he had tired of sitting out. The transport's destruction was a jab at Kaytrix, to remind him of Lord Khelveliz's power. The *Narvent's* destruction . . . that was pure spite.

Kaytrix glanced back to his screen. Several more transports were readying to disembark. No doubt Lord Khelveliz had figured out they were evacuating. With Kaytrix's forces spread thin, his gut told him things were going to escalate.

"Connect me with the other starship commanders." He left his seat to gaze out the viewport.

He studied the Nevo lord's poised ship. He could not allow the Nevo to destroy more transports while the battle occupied the Archarian fleet's attention.

"Sir, commanders are live," Satki said.

"Commanders," he said. "Our transports are becoming targets as our blockade weakens. Three vessels are readying to leave. I need everyone to form a tighter formation for their safe passage. Now!"

Satki confirmed the ships received the message.

Kaytrix waited, nervously watching Lord Khelveliz's ship, as the ships repositioned themselves. Thankfully, he didn't make a move.

"Kersa, watch Lord Khelveliz. If he so much as moves or charges weapons, I want to know."

"Yes, sir!" she responded.

There was a tense moment as the transports left the planet. He held his breath, waiting, watching Lord Khelveliz. The transports opened portals and jumped to their destination without a scratch. He was relieved, but there were many more to go.

Both sides continued to lose ships. The last of their fleet banded together, but their ability to stand fast waned as the battle reached a crucial turning point.

They were on the threshold of destroying two enemy ships, which could put the odds in their favor. The Nevo ships kept darting in and out of the battlefield, delaying their destruction and causing extensive damage to the Archarian fleet. The only thing that held Kaytrix back from pursuing them was the need to protect the planet and transports.

"What's the condition of the evacuation?" He had had enough of the Nevo toying with him.

"The admiral just sent an update," Levro shouted. "More transports are getting ready to leave with many civilians still traveling through the arkross. There are millions in need of transport and because of debris from the battle, we've lost several ships."

He faced a hard decision. He could hold his ground and lose an opportunity, or he could sacrifice the protective barrier they held around the planet to tip the scales in their favor.

"Order our closest sister ship to fill our blockade position," he said. "Nat, see those Nevo ships?"

"The annoying ones?" she growled.

"Yes. We're going to turn them into ashes." He projected fearlessness, but his bones quivered.

"Finally," she said.

The *Ro'arck* surged forward and overcame the first Nevo ship in moments. Detecting their approach, the Nevo vessel wove in and around debris, trying to lose them. Nat piloted the *Ro'arck* around the obstacles with ease, working to get a clean shot.

"Drozah, get ready," Kaytrix cautioned. "Open fire!"

Blue plasma ripped from the gun ports along with their improved missiles, striking the Nevo ship. It tore apart the shields, exposing the metal beneath. The ship heaved and buckled from the sudden heat melting through to its core.

Drozah fired relentlessly, a warrior cry erupting from his jaws.

The enemy was so close that Kaytrix perceived their shields rippling, signaling weakness. A stream of bullets flew through space at the precise moment the shield rippled, passing through the failing energy barrier and into the ship's metal. The Nevo ship succumbed to the attack and exploded, sending a shock wave through the carnage of the battlefield.

Drozah howled delightedly.

"Sir!" Kersa called. "My sensors detect Lord Khelveliz powering his engines and charging weapons. He's attacking!"

"Get us back in formation," Kaytrix growled. His jaw tightened. He should have known the attack would provoke him.

Nat guided the *Ro'arck* to the blockade when a barrage of weapons fire tore from Lord Khelveliz's ship, destroying several transports and their escorts. Lord Khelveliz then targeted several ships in their blockade, his powerful weapons tearing through them.

Kaytrix fell to one knee. That was the last straw. Fear kept him from pursuing Lord Khelveliz earlier; he thought he could buy them time to escape. It was all an illusion. Any decision made from fear was an unwise decision, a lesson learned too late.

"Tell the other ships to stay in formation," he ordered. "We will face Khelveliz alone."

Nat took immediate evasive action, dodging the swell of weapons fire by banking. The *Ro'arck* soared over her sister starships as she avoided the incoming fire and headed straight for Lord Khelveliz's ship.

He gripped his chair as they continued to provoke Lord Khelveliz. Their new missiles ripped through his heavy shields and blasted against his hull. Their impact had little effect against the heavy metal.

Over the comm, Satki shared their fellow commanders' voices. Panic was setting in for them at the blockade as the Varanus moved in, targeting the weaker sister ships and penetrating the barrier.

"Hold your ground! We have more transports to go!" Kaytrix encouraged. He could not have the commanders losing their remaining hope. There was still a chance that they could make it through this battle.

Then it happened.

Khelveliz's ship overtook the *Ro'arck* in a quick burst of speed, bolting past them and the blockade. He was heading toward their planet.

In the blink of an eye, the Nevo lord attacked their planet's anti-air defense system and their leaving transports. His powerful weapons pierced through the shields, shredding their metal hulls. He then targeted the weakest of their fleet the surviving ships broke apart in panic.

"Stay in formation," Kaytrix urged. "Concentrate fire on the closest enemy ships. Let nothing get to Archaria!" It was hopeless to stay in formation, but they couldn't survive if they broke apart.

"Sir, the ships in the blockade are falling to pieces. It is either them or Archaria," Levro shouted, turning to look at him. His sweaty face glowed in the flashing lights of the bridge deck.

Kaytrix could see that the young officer didn't want to give up. He spared a look at Archaria and immediately regretted it. Plumes of smoke rose in the planet's atmosphere. Archaria was under a full-scale attack from Khelveliz's fleet. What was left of their anti-air turrets hopelessly littered the atmosphere with a spray of bullets, attempting to destroy any ships in their path.

People continued to evacuate through the arkross and transports. They were counting on them to hold the line so they could make it to safety.

What other way to embrace the calling of the Warrior clan than to die in battle protecting his people?

He glanced back at his fleet. Most of them floated in space. Debris from their wreckage spread in an array of disheveled pieces. Several ships remained in formation, struggling to stay in the fight. The Archarian blockade was incapacitated.

If I am breathing, he reminded himself. The fight would continue.

"Inform the admiral to get as many people as he can to safety. We'll hold Lord Khelveliz's attention for as long as we can."

"Yes sir," Satki acknowledged.

The last of their fleet joined together from the wreckage of the battlefield and continued the fight. Beyond them, transports disappeared through the wisps of their portals.

"Target Lord Khelveliz and let him know we're still here," Kaytrix stated.

Missiles danced from the gunports and hit their target, damaging Lord Khelveliz's ship. Lord Khelveliz bore down on them with great speed.

"He's coming around to face us!" Levro announced.

Kaytrix stood and tightened his fists. The moment had come. "Prepare to fire everything we have, Drozah," he ordered. With the inevitable known, the sting of fear disappeared.

Lord Khelveliz attacked the *Ro'arck*. It lurched under the sudden fire, alarms wailing and drowning the bridge with flashing red lights.

The *Ro'arck* went into a nosedive. Nat pulled back on her controls to bring the ship to a sudden stop and Khelveliz's ship soared passed them. Nat thrust her controls forward in pursuit of him.

"Return fire!" Kaytrix called.

Drozah howled as they pelted the enemy's shields.

Nat held the *Ro'arck* on Lord Khelveliz's tail when the cannon on his ship swiveled, targeting them. Before the crew could prepare themselves, the main cannon fired. Two of the blasts missed as they flew between, but the last one hit hard.

"Sir, our life support has taken a serious hit," Levro shouted, his eyes wild with fear.

"Let's get above that main cannon," Kaytrix barked. The *Ro'arck* struggled to gain speed.

The enemy circled around and attacked again. Green fire raked the *Ro'arck's* hull, creating multiple explosions.

"I've lost an engine!" Nat said.

The Nevo ship overcame the *Ro'arck*, slowing to match their failing speed. Blasts of energy filled their view, tossing the *Ro'arck* to and fro. The enemy continued to circle around the weakening ship. Nat did her best to avoid the attacks, but she could not dodge every blast with a lost engine.

Further blasts hit the ship, tossing it aside. Then three large, concentrated cannon strikes hit the *Ro'arck*. The energy pierced their shields, carving hot plasma holes through the ship's structure. Atmosphere vented through the gaps and the ship started losing power. Warnings wailed in protest of the damage. Each holo-screen flashed a red warning to abandon ship.

Kaytrix sensed the crew's panic. Within moments, life support ceased to operate, and the remaining ship's systems slowly failed.

"Engines and navigations are offline! Other systems are failing. We're venting atmosphere!" Lieutenant Levro said.

"Get to the escape pods!" Kaytrix said. He ushered the crew to the exit. Lord Khelveliz was recharging his main cannon. They had to hurry.

Another blast hit the ship, tearing through it with ease. The impact flung Kaytrix over the length of the bridge. He lifted his gaze to see his crew recovering from the attack.

"Everyone to escape pods! *Now!*" he said. Panic was overtaking him as the adrenaline from the fight left his body. He gasped between breaths as he toiled to stand, weak from the lack of air to breathe.

The bridge crew scrambled. Nat and Drozah were leaving their stations when another round of weapons fire hit the *Ro'arck*.

The blast knocked Kaytrix off his feet and sent him flying through the stations. Sparks flew from the consoles. His breathing became ragged as he supported himself with an arm, trying to stand and assess their situation. Blood from his cut brow ran into his eyes. The warmth made his stomach churn as he peered through the mangled rubble. The bridge was a maze of fire, strewn metal, and mechanical parts.

His heart sank as he glimpsed Drozah pinned to a console by metal, his massive face buried in the shattered surface of a terminal.

Kaytrix ground his teeth, trying not to weep, when a noise caught his attention. Where was Nat? Did she make it out? As he searched for her, he wished selfishly that the groans were from another crew member and not from his beloved childhood friend, a friend that he cared for in other ways.

He struggled over the floor in search of the sound when he froze. Across the bridge, near the front of the vessel, a piece of metal lay across a person, exposing a delicate hand.

Hope and dread budded together in his soul, choking him of air. He dragged himself through the wreckage to investigate as sparks flew into his face. He reached the lower level of the bridge and, with the last ounce of his strength, pushed the metal sheet aside.

Tears fell from his eyes, betraying the feelings of his heart. There lay Nat, her eyes closed. A cut on her forehead drowned her beauty in a trail of blue blood.

"Nat!" he choked, kneeling beside her.

Blood pooled around her body. He braved a look behind her, and the harsh reality of her condition hit him. Metal had struck her back, piercing her vital organs.

Nat groaned again, this time struggling to open her eyes. "Sorry, Kaytrix," she said weakly, tears brimming in her eyes. "I should have acted sooner." She struggled to breathe. Her body was losing blood at an alarming rate.

"D-don't be ridiculous." He brushed her burgundy curls out of her face. He couldn't save her.

"I need to tell you something," she breathed again, every word a feat as her eyes focused on him.

"Don't speak. Save your energy," he begged, holding her hand as she looked into his eyes.

She smiled, blood saturating her teeth. "I love you, Kaytrix. Always have."

He let his tears fall. "I love you too, Nat. I wish I would have told you sooner."

Nat reached a hand to his face. "I always knew." She smiled. She took another breath, and her eyes shined their last spark of life.

Kaytrix's heart broke as grief welled inside of him. Tears stung his face as he loosened the clasp of his cloak and placed it over her. Her death crushed his soul.

Mac. Nat. Drozah. His parents. The crew. Archaria. Their alliance. The *Ro'arck* . . . Everything he had ever known and valued, taken from him. His grief was too much to bear.

Kaytrix closed his eyes, willing for this to be the last time he ever experienced fear, failure, or sorrow. He was done losing. The last thing to give up was his life. He waited for the ship to tear apart, to be destroyed by Lord Khelveliz, when a console near him activated, its chirp distinct.

He scoffed, recognizing it as the communications terminal. Ironically, it was one of the few systems left functioning.

Was it the Shargan queen with T'vos coming to his aid? He reached for his comm and opened the channel. This was the last shred of hope his heart could spare . . . Disappointment locked his face in a scowl as Lord Khelveliz appeared. The Nevo flashed his eyes in a glowing hue of neon green pride.

"Commander Torex," his sibilant voice hissed. "You have lost many battles, but your greatest tragedy is failing to protect your people. And now they will burn, like my race burned."

Kaytrix gazed at Lord Khelveliz, his brow furrowed in anger. This conversation could go one of two ways. He could listen to the Nevo gloat, or he could use his last weapon: time.

"You are right, I failed, but you missed one important detail," he said, each word a struggle. He held up his index finger and took another breath, dragging out the moment.

Lord Khelveliz scoffed, sending a mist of air through his grated mouth. "And what's that?" He crossed his arms.

"My people are not dead. One day, Archaria will return, and we *will* prevail against you!"

Lord Khelveliz hissed again, slamming a fist as he rose from his seat. The sound of his anger filled the ship and grated on Kaytrix's ears. It was the reaction he was hoping for—the reaction of fear.

Lord Khelveliz seethed. "Your arrogance is your true enemy, *Archarian*. Do not think I will end your pathetic existence. I have far greater plans for you, the likes of which will disgrace your race for generations to come! And as for your fellow Archarians, no matter where they hide, I will not rest until I find them. And when I do, I *will* destroy them! That is my promise to you, *Commander*!" He pointed a metal finger at him through the hologram.

Kaytrix punched the console, ending the transmission. Whatever Khelveliz threatened, his death was inevitable.

A wave of anger washed through Kaytrix as he struggled to breathe. He wished he could have done more to help his people. How come giving his life didn't feel like enough?

The computer beeped fervently, signaling that Lord Khelveliz's weapons were locking onto the *Ro'arck*.

Kaytrix gazed out the nearest broken viewport as the surrounding ship sparked and wailed warnings. There, his home world rotated. He remembered his father and his ma.

"I won't make it home this time," he said.

It was wrong to die this way, to give up so easily. There had to be something he could do. *If I am breathing, I am fighting*, he reminded himself.

Breathing.

The word set him free. He remembered behind each station on the bridge they stored emergency air canisters. If he could get to one, he'd have the strength to find a way to destroy Lord Khelveliz.

He struggled to stand and ignored the shooting pain through his body. He wobbled to his command chair, locating a cartridge of air and locking it into place on his armor. His helmet activated, allocating the air to his body. Oxygen rushed to his lungs and filled them.

Everything was offline because of the power outage, but there was one system separate from the others that would still be operational: the firing mechanism of the weapon's loader.

If there was a round of weapons loaded, he could release them at a target. Kaytrix reached over the armrest of his chair and activated his holo-screen. The computer glitched, but the screen projected. There were four improved missiles loaded in the chamber and ready to go. That was enough to cause severe damage.

His screen beeped—the *Ro'arck* was being targeted again. He needed to hurry. He lined his eyes up with the targeting grid, and the red lines shone bright, locating a perfect target: a Nevo ship. Through his viewfinder, the Nevos' shields rippled.

"Focus . . ." He breathed. The ship fell apart around him. Metal groaned, snapped, and popped. The cool vacuum of space seethed through the hull of the *Ro'arck* in the wake of Khelveliz's weapons as the weakened shields failed.

Kaytrix squeezed the trigger.

The missiles surged from their ports and whirled through the wreckage as they sought the unsuspecting Nevo ship.

The Nevo ship erupted, its explosion like fireworks to celebrate Kaytrix's servitude as an Archarian commander. It wasn't an ideal send-off to his death, but a damn send-off, nonetheless. He imagined Lord Khelveliz screeching in madness. The daydream was satisfying but short-lived when a metal panel struck him from behind and fractured his helmet.

By default, the helmet deactivated, leaving him exposed to space as the ship fell apart around him. The coolness of space viciously sucked the last of his life from him, but just as death began, everything was quiet.

Kaytrix opened his eyes to complete darkness.

No light.

No sound.

A dampness clung onto each breath he took. His hands and feet went numb. Was this the afterlife?

Then he felt it.

The same electric shock when Queen Rayla touched his hands surged through his entire body. His eyes drooped. He forced his eyes open to stay awake, but the sensation was too powerful to overcome, and against his will, he lost consciousness . . .

EPILOGUE

Commander Torex's ship exploded, the great flare blinding Lord Khelveliz for a second. In the background of the ship's destruction, the planet Archaria burned.

A feeling of victory swelled in his chest. It was just as he promised the Archarian, but his revenge was far from complete.

"Lord Khelveliz," one of his lieutenants said. "The transfer is complete, and the item is secure as requested."

Khelveliz hissed, excitement reverberating through his mechanical parts. At last, he could give this order with nothing standing in his way.

"Exterminate the Archarians. Leave nothing standing," he said, clenching his fist. An evil cackle left his throat as his fleet decimated the Archarian world. Finally, his revenge was complete. He continued chortling. He enjoyed witnessing the Archarians' destruction, his plans to end them coming to fruition.

"My lord, we have lost our remaining ship," one of his bridge soldiers informed him.

"What?" Khelveliz couldn't believe it. With the mighty power in his large mechanical frame, the Nevo lord flew over his command panel to peer through the viewport.

Anger grew inside him, rising, raging, until he emitted a screech that would penetrate every soul on the ship. This was an immense loss.

"Are there any survivors? Their shields should have spared them," he insisted, his voice grating with desperate hope.

"No, my lord. No life forms survived the blast." The soldier waited, seeming to expect a hit for delivering the news.

Khelveliz continued to seethe, his rage deepening as his green orbed eyes raked over the remains of Kaytrix's ship and his burning planet. The dimly lit bridge worsened his hatred and soured his victory. His lost ship possessed valuable soldiers, the last of their kind. Repercussions of the loss overwhelmed Khelveliz. Had it been worth it?

He reflected on his prize and the finality of his revenge. He imagined the Archarians' horrific screams, their immense agony . . . The justice of their ruin. Everything he had suffered, he'd make them suffer tenfold.

"My lord, what are your orders?" asked his second in command.

Lord Khelveliz reveled in the Archarians' destruction. Once a planet of life, now transformed into a wasteland of billowing smoke and fire. His revenge was not as sweet as he had envisioned, but it wasn't over yet.

The last words of the commander burned in his mind. There were transports leaving the planet, and that meant Archarians were alive. He would turn the galaxy on them, to hunt and kill every one of them with no allies to spare them from his wrath.

A moment passed, and his hollow heart renewed with a vengeful purpose.

"Take us back to Cordabo," he hissed.

A misty green portal opened before them. Like the monster he had created her to be, his pride and joy plowed through to Cordabo.

The planet waited below, its darkness a likeness to his first home, Kohmitz. Cordabo teemed with technology and life forms, rich with enough ore deposits and resources to start anew. It held great promise for him and his plans, like O'ber once had.

He submerged his hands in a soft, gel material in his console. A green light emitted from the gel upon activation. Around him on the bridge, lights along the floor flashed the same color—a silent message for his crew to prepare to leave. His soldiers stood by, ready to unload his newest victims and deliver it to his scientist, Vhulse.

As the ship neared the planet's surface, he prepared to land. What did Vhulse discover in his tests? The scientist promised to have results. Now more than ever, those findings meant more than their future—they determined their survival. Khelveliz seethed as his doubt bubbled inside. The news better be promising, or else.

The ship landed, and he navigated through dark halls with ease to the ramp of the vessel. He approached the cargo doors where his soldiers waited, the victims of his sieges in their hands. Fear widened their eyes.

Amusement replaced his doubt. The battered and bleeding life forms fought, screamed, and wailed at their captors as if they could escape the sheer power of the army he alone had created. The cargo doors opened then, and the ramp lowered onto the humid planet.

The screams intensified as the soldiers dragged their victims off the ship and toward the laboratory. Their flesh and bones were mush in the soldiers' iron grips, and they left a trail of blood in their wake. Their echoing screams across the dark space left him feeling energized.

"My lord," Vhulse greeted, approaching from farther up the landing pad.

Khelveliz glared at the scientist, distrust permeating through the cracks of his metal armor. His body angled defensively, ready to unleash an attack. "You best have good news, Vhulse," he threatened.

The scientist halted his advance at the warning. "I am sorry, my lord . . ."

There was a moment of silence as they eyed each other.

Khelveliz grew impatient. "Well, what is it?" he demanded.

Vhulse hesitated. "I am afraid we have made a grave mistake," Vhulse said, his hands fumbling.

Khelveliz narrowed his eyes at Vhulse, his mind processing the implications of his voice. "Continue."

"My lord, we cannot successfully replicate our symbiosis with other hosts . . ." Vhulse said, taking a step back.

Lord Khelveliz twitched, his head buzzing. Rage reached its peak in his body, taking his anger to an unknown extreme. His entire body resisted the urge to lash out at Vhulse.

"Speak plainly!"

Vhulse's hands trembled, and he dropped the screen containing the vital information. "H-h-here," he said, picking up the screen and passing the tablet to him.

He snatched the display and glared at Vhulse, trying to decide whether he should hit him now or later. He swiped through the holographic material with his sharp, taloned fingers. As he read the results of each report, he flipped through the information quicker.

"What is this?" he fumed.

Each report ended the same.

FAILED.

FAILED.

FAILED.

The results of the tests were failures. Each and every one.

"You mean to tell me—"

"Yes," Vhulse said. "We needed the Archarians, my lord. The continuance of our race depended on it."

The news was ironic. "What can we do?" Khelveliz asked, thrusting the report back into Vhulse's face. He had never dreamed that his ultimate vengeance would be his undoing.

"I have a plan," Vhulse said. "But it involves your prize."

Khelveliz gazed at his ship as his soldiers unloaded the canister carrying his war trophy. Inside, the hint of a silhouette.

His soldiers stood it in the planet's glittering darkness.

"NO!" he screeched. "He is not to be *your* experiment. There are others, others that escaped. Do whatever it takes to find them," he said defensively. What nerve Vhulse had to ask for his prize!

"That will take too long, my lord. We must be swift if we are—"

"Enough heckling!"

A moment passed as he considered the scientist's words. "If he dies by your hands . . ." he growled.

"He won't. My procedures will only bruise his outer tissue. In his state, he won't even know I am stealing his DNA and other key bodily fluids. If this works, sustainable hosts will never be a worry again," Vhulse said, a hint of pride in his voice.

Khelveliz snatched him by the throat and brought him close to his face. "Failure is not an option, Vhulse," he snarled. "This is your mission until you succeed, or until you *die!*"

Khelveliz threw Vhulse to the ground. He couldn't believe he was risking his future on the experience of a lower-caste Nevo. It was unfortunate that he had no choice.

He glared back at the still figure in the frozen liquid. It was as if the commander knew. Is that why he didn't retreat from battle?

The commander's frozen gaze seemed to mock him, but he hadn't had the last laugh yet. A world of pain was waiting for him. He just didn't know it.

ACKNOWLEDGMENTS

I would like to thank my husband, Steve, for the love and support he gave while this book was being written. Also big thanks to my dad, stepmom, and sister who always encouraged me and lifted me in my spirit.

To my friends, thank you for the everyday kind words of encouragement and the "what's next" questions.

Thank you to my beta reader, Gareth Matthews. You helped me out of my shell of fear.

To my Advanced Review Copy (ARC) team. Thank you for your time and energy in helping me see this project through. I owe you a lot of gratitude.

To my development editor Aubry Bennet and my copyeditor Brenna Bailey-Davis of Bookmarten Editorial, thank you for your strong encouragement, suggestions, and guidance on this project.

About the Author

Ericka Evren is the author of the *Archarian* series, a sci-fi space adventure that delivers emotional gut punches and challenges the deeper meaning of heroism and morality. She attended college for Early Learning and Childcare and now teaches at a preschool where she gets to be a big kid daily. Ericka wrote her first story at thirteen and published her debut novel, *Mission of the Ro'arck*, in 2022. She and her husband live in Alberta, Canada, with their two tabby cats, where they enjoy camping, family time, and nature.

Connect with her on social media: @erickaevrenauthor

Find more about Ericka and her books at: erickaevren.com

Connect

STAY UP TO DATE

If you loved the story and want to see what happens next, consider joining my monthly newsletter. There you will get one-on-one interactions with me, opportunities to become an ARC reader, sneak peaks to future projects, and much more! You can sign up for it by scanning the QR code below.

Newsletter Sign Up

THANK YOU

Thank you for reading my book! I can't tell you how much I appreciate it. It's readers like you who are vital for indie authors. Good reviews are also vital for indie authors and help readers find new adventures to experience.

If you enjoyed this book, would you help me reach more sci-fi loving readers by taking a minute to leave it a review? I can't tell you how over-the-moon I would be!

Below is a convenient to the best places to leave a review and help readers find a new sci-fi adventure to enjoy.